SURG

Having lost his memory and broken his arm in a car accident, aspiring surgeon Chris Felgate takes a temporary job in a group practice while he recovers. And there he meets Nurse Nicola Craven— who seems to know more about him than he does himself!

SURGEON IN WAITING

BY
CLARE LAVENHAM

MILLS & BOON LIMITED
15–16 BROOK'S MEWS
LONDON W1A 1DR

*First published in Great Britain 1985
by Mills & Boon Limited*

© Clare Lavenham 1985

*Australian copyright 1985
Philippine copyright 1985*

ISBN 0 263 75053 1

Set in 11½ on 12½ pt Linotron Times
03–0885–44,000

*Photoset by Rowland Phototypesetting Ltd
Bury St Edmunds, Suffolk
Made and printed in Great Britain by
Richard Clay (The Chaucer Press) Ltd
Bungay, Suffolk*

CHAPTER ONE

'WHEN'S THE great day, Nurse?' Mrs Stanton asked chattily.

She was talking to take her mind off having her stitches out, Nicola guessed that without much difficulty. This patient was a newcomer to Moresham and couldn't be expected to take much interest in the marriage plans of the doctor's niece. Nearly everyone else in the village must know the wedding was on Saturday.

Nicola carefully drew out the last stitch from a gash caused by a slipping carving knife. They dealt with a lot of those sort of minor accidents at the surgery for it was so much easier to visit the local doctor than to drive five miles to the Accident Unit at Debenbridge General Hospital.

'It's quite soon,' she said in answer to the question. 'Only another three days.'

'I expect you're ever so excited, dear. Got your dress and everything all ready?'

Was she excited? If she were honest the answer must be, 'No, not exactly.' But that was only because she had known Steve Paynton for such a long time. He had been the boy next door when they lived in Debenbridge and when Nicola and her mother moved to Moresham, to occupy the flat over the surgery, they had continued to see a lot of each other.

And now they were to be married.

Looking down at the modest diamond on her third finger, Nicola felt a rush of tenderness. Steve was hard up and at the moment actually out of a job, but he was usually full of grand plans for the future, and perhaps, with her to help him, he might be able to make something out of his life.

The little woman with untidy grey hair was looking at her curiously, obviously wondering why she was taking so long to reply. Hastily, Nicola recalled her wandering thoughts.

'There's so much to do before a wedding, even when it's a quiet one, and I think some of the excitement gets overlaid. But I'm very happy, naturally.'

When the patient had gone she looked into the waiting room to make sure there was no one else there, and automatically began to pick up scattered magazines and children's toys. As she finished her task Mrs Robson, one of the part-time receptionists, called out to her.

'Coffee's ready, Nicola. I reckon you could do with it!'

'You can say that again.' Nicola crossed the large tiled hall and went into the office. 'What a morning!'

'I sometimes think we're busier in summer than in winter. Of course, Moresham's growing so fast—turning into a real dormitory village— and the doctors have got more than they can comfortably cope with.' Mrs Robson smoothed back a lock of unnaturally black hair. 'I don't know how we're going to manage while you're on your honeymoon.'

'I shall be back on Monday evening, for goodness' sake! I'm only going away for a long weekend and after that it will be business as usual.'

Unconsciously a small sigh escaped her. It would have been so wonderful if she and Steve had been moving into a real home of their own instead of occupying two rooms in the large flat upstairs and sharing the kitchen and bathroom with her mother.

'I must go.' She finished her coffee and stood up. 'I've got to have an early lunch and then drive into the city to fetch my dress.'

'Don't forget your post-natal clinic at three o'clock.'

'Of course I shan't forget it! It's the one I enjoy most of all.'

'Maybe this time next year you'll have a baby of your own,' Mrs Robson said coyly.

Nicola smiled and kept her thoughts to herself. Steve didn't want to have children just yet, not until he had found a job and they were living on their own.

'I suppose some people might think it would be better not to get married until I'm working,' he had said with a tinge of bitterness. 'Like your mother, for instance. She hasn't exactly been enthusiastic about our moving into the flat.'

'That's not fair!' Nicola was indignant. 'Why, she even helped me with the redecorating of our rooms. I'd never have got it done in time if she hadn't. We did decide rather suddenly to fix up our wedding—remember?'

'Of course I remember.' He kissed the tip of her nose and rested his cheek against hers.

It felt rough and she wondered whether he had shaved that morning. Steve was fair-skinned and sometimes lazy about that sort of thing, just as his untidy light brown hair was frequently allowed to grow rather too long. He took after his mother, who was a happy-go-lucky sort of woman with a carelessly optimistic outlook on life.

Before going out that afternoon Nicola looked into the two rooms prepared with such loving care. Both were large, as were all the rooms in the big old-fashioned house, and the sitting-room looked pretty and comfortable with its colour scheme of apricot and green against plain white walls. There were plenty of bright cushions and new curtains to tone with them, and the slight shabbiness of the furniture hardly seemed to matter.

In the bedroom the colours were similar, though more subdued. The double bed was the one which Nicola's parents had shared before the divorce which had ended an increasingly unhappy marriage. She stood looking at it now, absent-mindedly smoothing the brand new cover with a gentle hand. Next week she would be sharing this bed with Steve. Deliberately she set her imagination to work and was rewarded by quickened pulses. Dear Steve—she knew him so well that it seemed their marriage *must* be a success. There could be no surprises for either of them.

Shaking off her inertia, she went to her own room and changed out of the blue uniform dress she wore for work, substituting for it a pink flowered summer skirt and white blouse. Her uncle, Dr Hardwick, had provided her with a Mini when she came to work as nurse attached to the practice and she drove swiftly along the narrow country road which led to the dual carriageway. From there it was only a short distance to the outskirts of the city.

They were expecting her at the boutique and soon produced the softly draped wedding dress in self-patterned wild silk which had required taking in a little on the hips. It now fitted perfectly, Nicola was glad to note as she stared at herself in the long mirror, but somehow she didn't look like a bride with her shoulder-length wavy dark hair uncovered.

'I'll try the veil as well, please,' she said to the salesgirl.

It made all the difference. Through the misty gauze, wide grey eyes looked solemnly back at her and she seemed, all in a moment, to have acquired some of the magic and mystery of a veiled woman from the east.

'You'll make a beautiful bride, Miss Craven,' the girl said sincerely. 'Sometimes dark girls have a pale skin which doesn't look good with white, but you've got a lovely colour. I'm sure you'll look your very best on Saturday.'

'I hope so,' Nicola told her. 'From what I've heard, half the village intends to come and stare at me.'

'Are you very well known locally then?'

'Only because of being the nurse, and the doctor's niece. My uncle is giving me away and he's very much liked by his patients, hence the interest.'

'I would hate to live in a village, with everybody knowing everybody else's business and no hope of keeping anything private.'

'You get used to it. I've worked in Moresham for four years now and it doesn't bother me at all usually.'

'Perhaps that's because you've never wanted to keep something secret,' the girl commented.

Slightly nettled, Nicola shrugged and made no reply. A glance at her watch told her she ought to be on her way back and a few minutes later she left the shop, burdened by two elegant white and gold boxes.

As always she left the busy main road with relief and slowed down as she neared the village. There were two new housing estates to be passed and then the road widened and the old original village began, with its post office, miniature supermarket, antique shop and garage. The church stood aloof, up a lane and half-hidden by trees, and the doctor's house—as it was generally

called, though its real name was The Elms—
was at the end of the street, a square red-brick
building with a semi-circular drive.

Until four years ago it had really been the
doctor's house, but Dr Hardwick and his wife
had moved into something smaller and easier to
run, and the whole of the ground floor had been
turned into surgeries, with a small dispensary at
the back, while the upper floor became a self-
contained flat.

Nicola could see several cars outside as she
approached and she knew that some of the
mothers had already arrived. Entering by a side
door she ran quickly upstairs and changed into
her uniform again.

'Thank heaven you're here!' Sheila Browning,
another part-timer, fair-haired and still
youngish, looked out of the office with a pile of
cards in her hand. 'They're in good voice today.'

Nicola smiled as she listened to the crying of
babies, shouting of toddlers at play and the
general chatter of their mums coming from the
waiting room. 'They always are.' She took
the cards and looked into the room. 'Who's
first?'

For the next hour and a half she was totally
absorbed, advising, weighing, sometimes just
lending a sympathetic ear. She did not give her
wedding another thought until her mother returned from her job at the central library in
Debenbridge just before evening surgery.

'Was your dress all right?' Alison Craven

asked when Nicola appeared in search of a cup of tea.

Alison was a good-looking woman in her early fifties and very like her brother, James Hardwick. Both had abundant iron-grey hair and fine features, although Alison was much too thin. She was looking tired this afternoon and there were two lines of worry on her otherwise smooth forehead.

'Absolutely perfect,' Nicola told her enthusiastically. 'I tried the whole outfit and was completely satisfied.'

'I'm glad something is satisfactory.' Meeting her daughter's reproachful gaze, she added defensively, 'I'm sorry, dear, but you know how I feel about this wedding.'

'You've made it quite clear, Mum, but I thought we agreed not to discuss it any more.'

Alison sighed and poured herself another cup of tea. 'Is Steve coming this evening?'

Nicola shook her head. 'He's going over to West Codden on his motor bike to see a friend about something.'

'We haven't seen him since the weekend. That's most unusual.'

'Yes—well, I expect he's busy.'

'Doing what?'

'Packing up his possessions—clothes and all that—ready to move in here.' Nicola had flushed but held on to her temper. 'His mother wants his room for one of the other boys so she'll be keen for him to get everything transferred to our flat as quickly as possible.'

Her mother did not answer and by mutual consent they avoided the subject of the wedding for the rest of the evening. At nine o'clock the phone rang and Nicola jumped up to snatch the receiver. It would be Steve for sure.

But it wasn't.

'Hi, Nicky!' It was the clear high voice of Janet Martin, a staff nurse at Debenbridge General who was to be Nicola's bridesmaid. 'I thought I'd give you a ring just to make sure everything's okay for Saturday. My dress is really super, just the right shade of green for a blonde, and I can't wait to put it on. I've never been a bridesmaid before.' Her tone changed slightly. 'Somebody told me green is supposed to be unlucky at a wedding. Did you know that? I don't believe a word of it, of course.'

'My mother did mention it, but I didn't take any notice. It's one of my favourite colours and I knew it would suit you. Did you manage to get your off-duty changed all right?'

'Another staff nurse swopped with me and I'm free all day. What time do you want me to come over and help you dress?'

They chattered on happily and some of Janet's excitement seemed to travel over the wires to Nicola, so that by the time they rang off she was feeling much more in the right frame of mind for a bride-to-be.

She slept well and awoke in the morning still with that undercurrent of happy anticipation.

But once downstairs she forgot everything but the job in hand, although Dr Featherstone, her uncle's partner, reminded her of her special status when he came breezing in twenty minutes late.

'Got called out to an emergency before breakfast—a case of cardiac arrest.' He smoothed back his pale thinning hair and brushed an imaginary crumb from the generous curve of his waistcoat. 'How's the blushing bride then? Got an attack of pre-wedding nerves yet?'

'I'm perfectly okay, thanks.' Nicola forced a smile. 'And I've no intention of getting nerves. All that sort of thing is terribly old-hat.'

'Is it? I wouldn't know.' He beamed at her and went into his consulting room.

Dr Hardwick, already at work, had made no mention of the wedding at all. He shared his sister's views on the subject, as Nicola was well aware, but was better at keeping them to himself. A quiet man with occasional flashes of temper, he dealt methodically with his patients and then went off to do his morning round. Dr Featherstone followed soon after and Nicola began her tidying up.

She had no clinic today but there were a few calls she wanted to make and these occupied what remained of the morning. By the time she parked her car again outside the doctor's house it was nearly one o'clock.

She was crossing the hall on her way to the stairs when Mrs Robson looked out of the office.

'Could you hold the fort for a little while, Nicola? Sheila Browning isn't here yet and I particularly want to get away in good time. You don't mind, do you, dear?'

'Of course not. You dash off and I'll stay downstairs until she comes.'

'Thanks a lot.' Mrs Robson snatched up her handbag and then paused. 'There's a letter for you—came by the second post. It's got today's date on it which means it must have been posted in Debenbridge early this morning. It's wonderful what the Post Office can do sometimes, isn't it?'

Nicola took the letter with a smile and sat down at the desk, glancing at the envelope as she did so. Steve's untidy scrawl! What on earth could he be writing to her about? He was the sort of person who always reached out for the nearest phone when he wanted to communicate with someone at a distance.

With fingers that trembled a little—though she couldn't think why—Nicola opened the letter.

She read the first page quickly, drew a long shuddering breath of total disbelief and ran her eye hastily over the rest of it. Then she let it fall to the floor and sat rigid, her gaze fixed and unseeing while two spots of bright colour burned in her white cheeks.

It wasn't any good disbelieving. Steve meant every word of it.

'*Dear darling Nicky,*' he had written. '*You're*

such a sweet understanding person that I'm sure you'll forgive me for what I'm going to do. I've got this wonderful chance of making something of my life at last and I can't let it go. My friend at West Codden wants me to go in with him at his radio and TV business but it means sharing the flat over the shop and always being on the spot. As you know, West Codden is twenty miles from Moresham and I couldn't ask you to give up your work and come here, even if there was room, which there isn't—so I'm afraid the wedding is off, for the time being anyway. You can imagine what a heel I feel for letting you down like this practically at the eleventh hour, but at least there's still time to cancel all the arrangements.'

Cold and sick with shock, Nicola struggled to come to terms with it, even though her instinctive disbelief still fought against acceptance. She would never have dreamt it possible that Steve could do this to her.

And for such a weak sort of reason too. Some way could surely have been found out of the difficulty—unless, of course, it wasn't a reason at all but an excuse. Perhaps he just wanted a way out and couldn't think of anything better. But if that was the case, why didn't he say so?

Because he hadn't the courage. Knowing Steve as she did, the answer was as plain as though it had been written across the office wall. Steve had always hated unpleasantness and you couldn't have anything much more unpleasant than telling a girl you'd known for years that you didn't want to marry her only two days before the wedding.

Nicola's lip curled and she was suddenly burning with rage. With a furious gesture she tore the letter into little pieces and flung them into the wastepaper basket. Hearing Mrs Browning's car stopping outside, she fled from the office and raced up the stairs to the sanctuary of her bedroom.

The tears came then, cascading down her face in a stream that seemed as though it could never end. And when they ceased she felt drained of emotion and so utterly weary that she could only be thankful she had a free afternoon.

By the time her mother returned Nicola had recovered some of her poise and was able to give her the information in a flat, dull voice which hardly quivered.

Alison was horrified. 'I could *kill* that wretched boy! Not that you aren't well rid of him, but I expect it's hard to accept that at such a time.' She looked anxiously at her daughter's set face. 'Do you feel able to help with evening surgery or shall I tell your uncle you aren't well?'

'I'll manage.'

'If any of the patients mention your wedding, just smile—if you can—and say nothing. They'll hear the news soon enough.'

'That's what I'm dreading,' Nicola confessed. 'Everybody knowing I've been stood up practically at the altar—all the comments and curiosity and gossip. It's going to be horrible.'

'They'll soon forget. I don't suppose it'll even be a nine days' wonder.'

'If only I could escape for a few days, maybe I could come to accept that.'

Alison looked thoughtful. 'Perhaps it could be arranged. How about going to your grand-parents' in Yorkshire for the weekend?'

'*No!* They'd be sweet and kind and I wouldn't be able to bear it. I need somebody more abrasive, who wouldn't let me be sorry for myself.' A sudden idea struck her. 'I know—I'll ring up Anthea Jennings in Dorset and invite myself for the weekend. I'm sure she won't mind.'

Anthea was another nurse and had trained with Nicola and Janet at Debenbridge General. Then she had married a doctor and disappeared to a country practice. But they had always kept in touch and both girls had stayed with her a few times.

Nicola made the call as soon as surgery ended, using the downstairs phone. To her dismay an answering machine replied, telling her in imper-sonal tones that Dr and Mrs Jennings were on holiday and she should get in touch with Dr Woodgate . . .

He wouldn't be much use at healing a desper-ately wounded heart. Nicola's lips twisted into a wry smile. Suddenly another idea leapt into her mind and she sat very still and pondered it care-fully. The more she thought about it, the better it seemed—but there was one big snag. It would involve lying to her mother and she would hate that, but if Alison knew she was intending to go off entirely on her own she would be seriously worried.

Her mind made up, Nicola went back upstairs.

'It's okay,' she said briefly. 'I fixed it up and I'm leaving here early on Saturday morning. I shall be back on Monday evening as—as I originally intended.'

In the meantime there was Friday to be got through. She managed it somehow, though it seemed to go on for ever, and then there was only her packing to do and she would be free. As she thrust clothes into a small case Nicola felt, for the first time, a faint stirring of interest. It was intriguing to have no idea of her destination, just to drive until she felt like stopping. Who knew what it might lead to?

The answer was probably—loneliness.

She was hanging up her dressing-gown in the morning when she caught sight of her wedding finery. She couldn't leave it there, to greet her when she returned, and with a sudden savage gesture she tore it off the hanger. With teeth set, she bundled the beautiful dress and veil into a polythene bag and carried it downstairs with her case. She must get rid of it somehow, somewhere, and quickly.

That hateful object on the back seat had quite spoiled the sensation of release she had hoped to experience on making her getaway. Her mind fixed on one thing only, she drove slowly, looking about her for a litter basket—anything. But she was in the wrong sort of area and there was nothing suitable.

Desperate, she hesitated on a river bridge and then parked her car in a layby. It was still early and no one saw her walk back to the bridge, a bulky parcel in her arms. Reaching the parapet, she leaned on it for a moment, staring down into the brown water. Then, with sudden resolution, she flung the bag violently from her, and as it descended to the water below it seemed to her that it took with it all her hopes and dreams.

Blinded by tears, she turned away, stumbled a little and lurched straight into the path of an approaching car. There was a scream of brakes, a skidding noise and then a furious male shout.

'What the hell do you think you're doing? Trying to commit suicide?'

CHAPTER TWO

'ARE YOU all right?' the voice demanded, a shade less furiously. 'Good God—you're crying! What on earth's the matter?'

Nicola brushed her hand across her eyes and was mortified when it came away wet. 'Of course I'm all right,' she said crossly. 'I just didn't happen to see you coming.'

'Because you weren't looking. Of all the idiotic things to do—plunging into the road like that! You nearly gave me a heart attack.' A very large young man with tawny hair climbed out of the car, which was low, silver-grey and sporty-looking, and towered over her. 'You threw something in the river, didn't you?' he accused. 'What was it?'

She ought to tell him to mind his own business but he was a stranger—someone she would never see again—and it seemed simpler just to be truthful.

'My wedding dress,' she said defiantly. 'So what?'

He stared at her and one very small part of her mind noted that his eyes were a particularly brilliant blue with long curling lashes to match his hair. He had a lean, tanned face with strongly marked brows, a well-shaped if slightly over-prominent nose and a thrusting chin. He also had a slight accent of some sort.

'Do you make a habit of throwing your clothes into the river?' he asked incredulously. 'If so, I think you should give serious consideration to the little matter of pollution. And then there are the ducks. There are sure to be some on the water—swans too, perhaps. Have you thought that they may get tangled up in your wedding dress?'

Nicola stamped her foot. 'I suppose you think you're being very witty, saying silly things like that. Well, I don't think it's funny. It was a *new* wedding dress—I'd never worn it and I never shall now and—and—' Her voice broke and she couldn't go on.

'I see. At least, I don't really, but I'd like to.' He paused and then added quietly, 'Want to talk about it? If so, my car is at your disposal.'

'I've got a car. It's in the layby.'

He glanced at the Mini and she felt sure he was comparing it with his own much more exciting vehicle. 'I'm not sure I could fold myself up into that so you'd better get in this one and I'll park with yours.' He held the door open. 'Hop in.'

Nicola scarcely hesitated, in spite of all her mother's warnings about strange men in strange cars. Although she thought him the rudest and most overbearing young man she had ever come across, somehow she trusted him. Besides, she badly needed to talk to someone.

'Now,' he said, drawing up neatly behind the Mini and reverting to the peremptory tone he had used earlier, 'get on with it.'

And so she told him, pouring it all out—the bitterness and disappointment and the miserable sense of rejection. He listened without interruption, staring straight ahead down the empty country road.

'It sounds to me,' he said when she had finished, 'as though you're well rid of this guy.'

'I've already had all that from my mother,' Nicola snapped, 'and I don't want it from you as well.'

'Okay.' He sat frowning for a moment and then asked abruptly, 'Well? What's the next move?'

'Move?' She turned a bewildered face towards him.

'Give me patience! Listen, my girl, and try to understand what I'm saying. I don't think you're really a moron, though you're behaving like one.' He began speaking very slowly and carefully, as though to a small child. 'I'm trying to find out what your plans are. Are you on your way somewhere or were you just driving round aimlessly?'

On the verge of admitting the truth, Nicola thought better of it. Looking round wildly, her eyes alighted on a convenient signpost. 'I'm going to Sandbeach,' she said firmly, 'to spend the weekend by myself and get adjusted to what's happened.'

He studied her thoughtfully. 'Sounds a good idea, up to a point, but I think you may find it lonely.'

She shrugged. 'I can stand that.'

'Is Sandbeach a nice place?'

'I wouldn't be going there if it wasn't.' Nicola opened the passenger door. 'Thank you for listening to my troubles. I hope I haven't bored you too much.' He started to say something but she was out of the car in a flash. 'I'll be on my way now. Goodbye.'

He called out after her but she took no notice. She could feel him watching her as she got into her car and started the engine, but he made no attempt at pursuit. As soon as she reached the road she put her foot down hard on the accelerator. She had revealed her feelings to this total stranger more frankly than to her own family, and although she felt better for the experience she hoped she wouldn't ever meet him again.

For a time she followed the Sandbeach road without incident. And then, in her rear mirror, she saw a fast car approaching from behind, its silver body shining in the sunlight. It shot past her with a toot of recognition and disappeared round the next bend.

Nicola immediately slowed down. At the rate he was driving it seemed unlikely that they would have any further contact but it seemed safer to let him get well away. Accordingly she dawdled along at a modest thirty-five miles an hour, thankful that she was on a country road with little traffic and not the main road to Sandbeach. The other car seemed to have completely disappeared.

And then, as she rounded one of the many bends, Nicola saw it again. It was drawn up near the grass verge, dark skid marks showing that it had pulled up in a great hurry.

She had just enough time to notice that the car was empty when its owner came crashing through the low hedge and made an imperious gesture to her to stop. Something was evidently very wrong—one glance at his face told her that—and she obeyed at once.

'I hope you're stronger than you look,' he said tersely, 'because I need help—'

'What's happened?'

'You see that dead elm?' He pointed to a large tree towering above the hedge. 'Two boys were swinging on one of the branches and it broke and trapped one of them. I've sent the other off to phone for an ambulance and tell his parents, but I'd like to move the branch as soon as possible. The poor kid's in pain.'

Nicola scrambled through the hedge after him without another word. A boy of about ten with wide, frightened eyes lay on the ground, both his legs held fast by a massive piece of timber. He said in a trembling voice, 'Please—please—'

'Hang on, laddie, we'll soon get you out of there.' The untidy brown hair was smoothed with a surprisingly gentle hand, and Nicola received her instructions. 'We'll have to lift the branch clear—if we try to roll it we may do more damage. You take the lighter end and heave when I give the word.'

She bent willingly to her task, marvelling at the weight as her muscles took the strain. For a moment she thought she couldn't do it, but she set her teeth and called on her last reserves of strength. Slowly—very slowly—the branch was raised and laid down at a safe distance.

'Now let's have a look at those legs.' He ran his hands down the thin little limbs, displaying so much competence that Nicola decided he was either a trained first-aider or a doctor.

Both legs were badly bruised and lacerated, and one lay at an awkward angle and was probably broken. She was not surprised to be asked whether she had any rag in her car, and when she had fetched some and torn it into strips, the damaged leg was carefully immobilised by being tied to the other. After that the stranger took off his sweater and tucked it round the little boy, talking to him quietly as he did so.

'Treatment for shock?' Nicola suggested.

'Of course. I'm a doctor, by the way, in case you haven't guessed. Chris Felgate is the name. I'm British but my family moved to Canada eight years ago and I did my medical training there. I'm back in the UK for good now, I hope, and for starters I've landed a registrar's job at Debenbridge General Hospital, working with Mr Bradshaw. I'm hell-bent on surgery, you see.'

'You're lucky to get in with him,' Nicola said. 'He's an absolutely brilliant heart surgeon.'

'So I've heard. It seems strange he hasn't migrated to one of the big London hospitals.'

'He's got a heart condition himself and has to be careful.'

'How do you know that?' Chris asked curiously.

'It was common knowledge even when I was a student nurse at Debenbridge. My name's Nicola Craven,' she added hastily.

'So you're in the medical profession too, Nicola? That should make a bond between us.'

She raised her eyebrows but was spared from answering by the sound of the ambulance siren. The little boy was looking scared again and she devoted herself to reassuring him as best she could.

'I wish my Mum was here,' he said piteously.

'I expect she'll soon turn up at the hospital,' Chris told him. 'Perhaps even be there waiting for you.'

The ambulance men were kind and fatherly, and soon made their small patient comfortable. As they watched the vehicle drive away down the road, Chris turned to Nicola.

'It really does seem as though fate is determined to fling us together,' he observed.

'Does it?' For some reason her heartbeats had quickened slightly.

'Don't pretend you haven't noticed.' He smiled, his eyes very blue. After a slight pause he continued speaking in a slow, deliberate tone. 'I've been thinking that it might be a good idea for me to spend the weekend at Sandbeach too, just to keep an eye on you and make sure you aren't lonely. I haven't got anything particular lined up until Monday evening.'

'*What?* You've got a nerve!' Nicola gasped. 'Do you really think I would agree to spending the weekend with a total stranger?'

Chris grinned wickedly. 'I'm not proposing a dirty weekend, though I'm sure I'd find it very enjoyable. I don't think you're quite ready for that—yet.'

'Then what are you proposing?' she demanded.

'A perfectly respectable arrangement whereby we occupy separate rooms at the same hotel—or even different hotels if you insist—and spend our time in such innocent pursuits as walking, talking, maybe swimming . . . How about it?'

Nicola was silent. The suggestion was so fantastic that it might just possibly turn out to be a good idea. Keeping her end up with such an appallingly bossy young man might take her mind off things she wanted to forget. And if she found out she couldn't stand his male ego another minute, then she could pay her bill and slip quietly away.

'Okay,' she said abruptly. 'I'll agree to this crazy idea if you promise to keep all the rules.'

Even as she spoke she was appalled at herself.

Only a short time ago she had been hoping never to see him again. What on earth had come over her?

'Anything you like within reason,' he said cheerfully.

As she drove down the road and saw the silver-grey car following at a little distance, Nicola still couldn't believe it was really happening. But as the miles slipped away and she caught her first glimpse of a blue line across the horizon, her spirits lifted. The lonely weekend she had planned was turning into something of a challenge and the prospect was oddly stimulating.

Sandbeach was a small, quiet place where the season started late. Nicola drove straight to the front, vaguely remembering that there were several medium-priced hotels along to the right. Slowing down, she looked them over and picked out one called Belmont which had an extremely respectable air.

'Do you really want to stay here?' Chris joined her as she was getting out of her car.

'It looks very—suitable.'

'Suitable for what?' He raised one eyebrow and grinned.

Ignoring the question, she led the way into the entrance hall, which was red-carpeted and rather stuffy. The receptionist—who was young and pretty—looked at them with interest and gave them adjoining rooms with a slightly conspiratorial manner.

'We'll just get settled in,' Chris said, 'and then have some lunch.'

The weather was warm and sunny but Nicola felt too lazy to change out of her cream linen trousers and yellow T-shirt and put on a summer dress, so she was soon ready.

Chris was waiting for her downstairs and they lunched in the public bar of the hotel, which was hidden at the back, as though having no connection with the prim front. At his suggestion they went for a walk afterwards, first along the promenade and then on the cliffs, finding conversation easy, though they kept to general topics.

The exercise and strong sea air made them both sleepy and dinner in the formal dining-room, with its neat waitresses, was a quiet meal. As soon as she decently could, Nicola escaped to bed. Too tired for any more emotion, she was asleep within minutes.

She awoke to sunshine and the harsh crying of gulls, and for a moment couldn't think where she was. Recollection quickly flooded back, but it seemed no more substantial than the memory of a bad dream. She was conscious of neither happiness nor unhappiness and felt rather as though she were living in a vacuum.

The day followed the same pattern as yesterday, except that they took a quick dip in a rather chilly sea after Nicola had purchased something to wear from one of the holiday shops open on Sunday.

'Why didn't you get a bikini?' Chris asked

disapprovingly as he looked at the plain one-piece turquoise swimsuit.

'Because I already have two at home. It didn't occur to me to bring them.'

They were lying side by side on the beach, trying to pretend it was warm enough for sunbathing. Although their bare arms were not even touching, Nicola was suddenly aware in every fibre of her being of his masculine aura. Seen almost naked, he was a magnificent figure of a man, broad-shouldered and with a flat stomach and slim hips. He had, in addition, a most enviable all-over tan.

'Where did you get so marvellously brown?' she asked enviously.

'I'm just back from a tour which included sailing round some of the Greek islands. I arrived in England about three weeks ago, saw old Bradshaw and ordered myself a car and then went off on holiday. I only got back yesterday. The car was waiting for me and I planned to spend the weekend driving round and getting used to English traffic regulations. I'm due to start work on Tuesday.'

'I'm afraid you haven't done much driving,' Nicola said.

Chris rolled over and raised himself on his elbows, looking down at her with a half grin. 'Want me to say that the change of plan has been well worth it?'

'No, of course not.' Indignant, Nicola reached for her towel. 'You can lie there and freeze if you like, but I'm going to get dressed.'

'I'll do the same and then we'll go and get some coffee to warm you up.'

By now she was getting used to his bossy 'I know what's best for you, my girl' sort of treatment, and in a way she had even enjoyed it. It certainly made life easy to be so totally taken charge of. Most of the time she let him lead the conversation, with the result that she had learnt a lot about his life in Canada, his home and family and his ambitions for the future. He was crazy about surgery, he told her, and always had been. It was the luckiest possible break getting the job at Debenbridge.

He hadn't learnt so much about her because it was difficult to talk about her own life without mentioning Steve, since he'd been around in it for so long. And she didn't want to talk about Steve, not ever again.

But at dinner that night Chris deliberately steered the conversation in that direction.

'This time tomorrow you'll be home again, Nicola.' His blue eyes held her gaze. 'How do you feel about it?'

'I—don't know,' she admitted reluctantly.

'That's no sort of an answer. You can make a guess, surely?'

Her eyes dropped and she stared down at the bright red synthetic tomato soup in her plate. 'I think I'm more able to cope than I was yesterday, if that's what you mean.'

'I should hope so too after all the effort I've put

into standing you up on your own two feet again! But that wasn't entirely what I meant. The most important thing is how you feel about that guy who let you down; whether you've had the sense to realize that you were never really in love with him at all.'

'Not in love with Steve! Of course I was,' she said angrily.

Chris shook his head and continued in his most dogmatic tone. 'From what you poured out to me yesterday morning, you were sorry for the bloke and confused that emotion with love. He's out of a job, isn't he? A girl like you is just the sort to imagine she could work a miracle, bolster up his morale and all that, so he'd end up a completely different guy.'

'You don't know anything about it! How can you when you've never met him?'

'I'm pretty quick on the uptake,' Chris said complacently.

'And pretty conceited too—that's been sticking out a mile all the weekend. Who gave you the right to drag out my private emotions and cold-bloodedly dissect them?'

'Nobody,' he told her calmly, 'but it's obvious you needed to talk about Steve some time before you went home. You must have been badly muddled about the whole affair or you'd never have got yourself into the sort of situation where a man could behave towards you the way he did.'

'That's a load of rubbish!' Nicola flung at him, abandoning all pretence of eating. 'I couldn't possibly have guessed he'd do a thing like that.'

'Perhaps not, but where you went wrong was in agreeing to the marriage when all you felt was affection and pity.'

Her eyes diamond-bright with anger, she glared at him across the table. 'You're still at it, analysing me and my feelings. You ought to have been an analytical chemist instead of a doctor.'

'No, thank you. The work wouldn't appeal to me. I prefer dealing with human beings.' Chris studied her flushed face. 'If you're honest with yourself, Nicola, you'll admit that it's your pride which has suffered the biggest blow, not your heart. Humiliation can be very bitter but it's nothing like as bad as a broken heart.'

Nicola was silent as the hot colour faded, leaving her very pale. An elderly waitress appeared at her side and removed the soup plate, substituting roast beef and Yorkshire pudding and she looked at it with distaste. Resentment of Chris filled her to such an extent that there was no room for anything else.

With a sudden movement, she stood up, pushing her chair back so violently that it nearly overturned. 'I don't want any more dinner and I'm going up to my room,' she snapped. 'Good night.'

As she crossed the dining-room she felt sure that Chris must be staring after her in consternation, but when she looked back as she turned at the door he was calmly getting on with his dinner. He did not even give her a glance.

Her room felt stuffy and Nicola opened the window wider, letting in the wash of the sea and the sound of voices and passing footsteps. Out there, life continued as usual, but in her bedroom at half-past seven in the evening she was totally isolated and very much alone.

What on earth was she to do with the rest of the day? It was at least two hours before she could possibly go to bed.

Eventually she decided to have a bath, making it last as long as possible, and then put on her red velvet caftan and lay on the bed, listening alternately to the radio and the increasing noise from the bar, which was now drifting in at the window. Chris would be there, she supposed, enjoying himself talking to strangers and, no doubt, glad to be rid of someone whom he obviously regarded as neurotic.

Dusk came and Nicola switched on the bedside lamp. In spite of all the fresh air and exercise she had had, she still felt restless and mentally active. The conversation at the dinner table repeated itself endlessly in her head and her precipitate flight seemed increasingly foolish.

At nine o'clock there was a tap at the door.

Nicola jerked upright in bed and sat rigid, her heart pounding. A moment later the tap came again.

It was idiotic to ignore it. She slipped off the bed and crossed the room with bare feet. Her hand shaking slightly, she turned the knob and opened the door. Chris stood outside, his arms full. He was smiling and looked completely at ease.

'I knew you'd be hungry by now so I brought you chicken in a basket and a bottle of wine. I thought we could have a picnic.'

He came in without waiting for an invitation and put his burden down on the bedside table. 'Well, come on,' he said. 'I'm sure you're starving.'

It was true too, Nicola realised in surprise. The food was beautifully arranged and very tempting but there was far too much for one person.

'No way could I possibly eat all that,' she protested.

'So what? I can easily help you out and I intend to drink my share of the bottle, naturally.' He grinned at her, his eyes glinting in the lamplight. 'Let's get on with it, shall we?'

Nicola already felt light-headed and she didn't know what the wine would do to her, nor did she care. There was an extraordinary party atmosphere developing in the impersonal hotel bedroom and they talked and laughed as they had not done during the whole weekend.

But when they had finished and tidied up, Chris was suddenly serious.

'The therapy worked, didn't it?' he asked. 'You were angry with me at dinner but you didn't burst into tears. I think you would have done yesterday.'

'Not in public, I hope,' she hedged.

'Up here then.' He looked at her closely. 'I

don't see any traces of tears at all.'

'I didn't shed any, nor did I want to.'

'That's good.' They were sitting side by side on the edge of the bed and he moved closer, taking her unresisting hand. 'How about carrying the therapy a little farther? I'd like to send you back completely cured.'

Her heart was thudding so that she could hardly speak, but she managed to gasp, 'Oh, Chris—you—you promised—'

'I haven't forgotten, and if you want me to go away this minute then I'll go,' he said quietly. 'But I think it would be an awful pity not to stay a bit longer.'

And suddenly, overwhelmed by a strange recklessness, Nicola found that she thought so too.

CHAPTER THREE

'I'LL GIVE you a ring some time,' Chris said casually.

It was Monday evening and they had reached the point where their roads diverged. Nicola would cross the dual carriageway heading for Moresham and Chris would turn right towards the city. He would take possession of his flatlet at the hospital tonight and in the morning start work. She sensed that mentally he was already totally absorbed in the future, that for him the weekend had been nothing more than a way of passing the time.

'My number's in the book.' Her tone matched his but it was an effort.

'You gave it to me. Last night.'

'Did I? I'd forgotten.'

'Liar.' He laughed outright as she flushed indignantly. 'Be seeing you, Nicola. Take care and drive safely.' His lips brushed hers and then he got back into his car and drove off.

She watched the silver-grey streak as it turned the corner and roared away. In spite of what he had said she doubted if she would ever see it—or its owner—again.

Did she want to?

Afraid to search for an answer, Nicola restarted her own car and drove slowly in the direction of home. The nearer she got to the village, the more she dreaded the coming interview with her mother. It would be impossible to keep up the pretence that she had visited Anthea Jennings in Dorset, for there was no one quicker at detecting she was being deceived than Alison. Nicola would have to tell her at least something of the truth.

She was flung into it as soon as she arrived. Her mother heard her coming up the stairs and hurried out to greet her.

'You're looking so much better, dear.' The tone held surprise and relief. 'Not even tired after your long drive.'

It was a perfect opening and Nicola snatched at it.

'I haven't had a long drive. I—I changed my mind about going all that way and went to Sandbeach instead.'

Alison's finely marked eyebrows rose in amazement. '*Sandbeach?* But you don't know anyone there, do you?'

'No, I don't, but that didn't matter. I stayed at a small hotel and—and just had a lazy time.'

'To think you were only thirty miles away and I never knew it! You really should have rung up and told me your whereabouts. I might have wanted to get in touch with you urgently and I would have phoned Anthea, naturally. I suppose you remembered to ring and tell her you weren't coming after all?'

'Yes, of course,' Nicola said lightly and picked up her suitcase. 'I'd better go and unpack.'

'She must have thought it a bit odd, but I expect she made allowances under the circumstances. Weren't you terribly lonely, staying at Sandbeach all by yourself?'

'Not really. The weather was lovely and I walked a lot and even bathed yesterday morning.' Nicola paused in the doorway. 'Did—did Steve ring up during the weekend?'

'Goodness, no! I shouldn't think even he would have the nerve. I would have given him a piece of my mind if he had.' Alison went into the kitchen to plug in the kettle. 'Janet phoned,' she called over her shoulder. 'I told her you were with Anthea, of course, so you'd better put it right with her next time you see her.'

More lies. But it would be easier with Janet than it had been with her mother, though even that hadn't been too bad. In the meantime there would be the patients to face. They'd all know about the wedding fiasco by now, of course.

Nicola went downstairs in the morning with her head held high and a sort of determined calmness about her.

Mrs Robson said fervently, 'Thank goodness you're back—it was murder without you yesterday,' and made no reference to what had happened. In the waiting room the patients were equally reticent, though some of them rather overdid their friendly greetings.

Dr Hardwick gave her a searching look when

he came in and asked quietly how she was.

'I'm fine, thanks, Uncle,' she said brightly. 'I had a lovely lazy weekend and all I want now is to settle down to work again.'

'That's the spirit!' He smiled and touched her lightly on the shoulder. 'Nothing like hard work for taking your mind off your troubles.'

Dr Featherstone made no reference to the cancelled wedding. He was feeling sorry for himself because he had been on call all the weekend, had had his Sunday lunch interrupted and two broken nights.

'I'm always telling your uncle we should add another doctor to the firm,' he said to Nicola, 'but James is such an obstinate man. Just because we used to be able to manage okay he thinks we can continue to do so, in spite of the increase in patients.'

'Before you came he was on his own,' Nicola pointed out. 'He feels possessive about the practice and I suppose you can understand it.'

'Frankly, I don't understand it in the least.' Dr Featherstone sounded unusually disgruntled. 'I told James only yesterday that *he* may be prepared to work himself into the grave but I'm not.'

'What did he say?' Nicola asked curiously.

'Just that he hoped there wouldn't be any question of graves and personally he thrived on hard work.'

'He's been looking very tired lately,' she said thoughtfully.

'I've noticed that too.' He smoothed back his thinning hair. 'And I've certainly been feeling tired, whether I look it or not. I'll have another go at him when I get the chance.'

Nicola nodded approval. 'I feel sure you'll make your point in the end, Doctor,' she said, trying not to look at her watch. He was already late for his first apppointment.

Time began to gallop past at its usual speed. When the waiting room was empty she got out her car and drove to call on a few patients who, for one reason or another, needed her help in their own homes. It was inevitable that there should be some comments of a personal nature, but they were little more than a sincerely expressed word of sympathy and not hard to bear.

In the afternoon her uncle took her with him to visit a neurotic patient who was in bed with a multitude of complaints, largely imaginary.

'I'm terrified of the woman, Nicola,' he confessed with a wry smile. 'She's just the sort to con herself into believing I'd made a pass at her.'

She studied her distinguished-looking uncle with some amusement. He was so very sure of himself as a rule. 'That sort of thing is the GP's occupational hazard,' she reminded him. 'She's probably sex-starved and you *are* very handsome, you know.'

He snorted in disgust but did not look displeased. With Nicola present the visit was without incident, though she sensed the woman's disappointment. After that it was soon surgery time again and the day was almost over.

Wrapped round in the familiar routine, she kept her mind firmly on work and managed to hold Steve at bay. As for Chris, as the week slipped away and she heard nothing of him she told herself she hadn't really expected to anyway. No doubt he was now totally immersed in his new job and last weekend would have been nothing but an incident to him.

On Thursday evening the phone rang.

It had been strangely silent all the week and consequently the sudden insistent call caused Alison to glance uneasily at her daughter.

'I hope that's not Steve.'

'Shouldn't think so.' Nicola jumped up and went out on to the landing, her heart beating just a little faster.

She had not really expected it to be Chris and was surprised to find herself oddly disappointed when she heard Janet Martin's voice.

'I've been meaning to ring you all the week, Nicky. I do hope you're not too unhappy over that wretched Steve? I've been telling myself that from your point of view it was probably for the best, even though I was terribly upset about the wedding cancellation. How are you *really* feeling?'

'Not too bad, thanks.' Nicola took a deep breath. 'I think I somehow managed to come to terms with it during the weekend.'

'It was such a good idea to go off like that. How

did you find Anthea? It's ages since I saw her.'

'Well, as a matter of fact—' She plunged into her explanation.

Janet, who liked people around her all the time, was even more amazed than Alison had been. 'What an extraordinary thing to do! Weren't you dreadfully lonely?'

'You're not exactly alone at a hotel. There's always somebody to talk to if you feel like it,' Nicola said vaguely.

'I still think it was a most peculiar thing to do—but we can't all be alike, I suppose.' Janet changed the subject. 'Are you doing anything on Saturday morning?? I'm free until two o'clock, so perhaps we could meet for coffee and have a natter.'

Glad to have something organised for her, Nicola agreed at once and they arranged to meet outside their favourite coffee shop. During the following day she looked forward to the occasion and hoped she would manage not to give Janet even the slightest hint that the weekend had been anything out of the ordinary.

Debenbridge was always busy on a Saturday and Nicola had to park her car some distance from the rendezvous. It was a cool, breezy day and she walked briskly with her dark hair blowing back from her face.

Janet, standing outside the shop, watched her approach. 'It's easy to see *your* feet aren't killing you,' she said enviously.

'If that's supposed to mean I don't work hard—' Nicola began indignantly, but broke off as her arm was seized.

'Do let's hurry and get a table—this place gets so crowded. Besides, I've got something tremendously interesting to tell you and I've been saving it up almost ever since our phone conversation, so I shall probably burst soon.'

Aware that Janet was given to exaggeration, Nicola was not particularly impressed. But by the time they had collected their coffee and found somewhere to sit she was beginning to feel a faint stirring of curiosity. Janet's blue eyes were dancing and she really did look as though she had something interesting to say.

'Well, come on,' Nicola said. 'What's all this then?'

'It's quite a long story and I'll have to go back to last Tuesday. You know I work on an orthopaedic ward, well, when I went on duty that morning there was a new patient who'd been admitted late the previous evening. He'd been in a car crash and he was rather badly knocked about, but nothing serious. Cuts and bruises, a couple of broken ribs, a fractured left arm and quite bad concussion.'

Nicola knew exactly the sort of case she meant. Very painful and unpleasant for the patient but absolutely nothing to worry about.

'He didn't even know who he was at first,' Janet went on, 'but we got his name from the contents of his pockets. He was very confused for several days but when eventually he was able to ask intelligent questions about what had happened to him, Sister told me to get his personal possessions and return them to him.'

She paused to drink some coffee and Nicola waited. She couldn't imagine what all this had to do with her, but at the same time a nameless apprehension was slowly growing.

'Go on,' she said quietly.

'I'm coming to the really extraordinary part now. I fetched the man's wallet and papers and all that from a drawer in the office. They were in a polythene bag but it wasn't fastened and a piece of paper dropped out just as I was going into the ward. I couldn't help reading what was on it when I picked it up and it had *your* name and address written across it! *And* your phone number!'

Janet came to a full stop and gazed expectantly across the table. She was obviously waiting for a tremendous reaction of some sort, but Nicola was speechless with dismay. It just had to be Chris who had landed in the orthopaedic ward— but whatever could have happened?

Her patience at an end, Janet went rushing on. 'You can just imagine how astonished I was! I didn't think there was any man in your life except Steve. You've never even mentioned anybody called Chris Felgate.'

'I—I hardly know him.'

'Oh, come off it, Nicky! Why'd he have your phone number then?'

'He asked me for it quite casually. I don't suppose for a moment he would ever have used it.' Seeing that Janet's exasperation was about to boil over, Nicola hurried on. 'I told you I went to Sandbeach last weekend. Well, Chris happened to be staying at the same hotel and we—got talking. That's all.'

It wasn't all, not by any means, and Janet plainly had serious doubts on the subject, though she controlled herself to the extent of merely raising skilfully darkened eyebrows.

'Don't you want to know what had happened to the poor chap?'

'Of course I do. Did you say he had the accident on Monday evening?'

'That's right. It was at that big roundabout not far from the turning to Moresham. The police said he went right instead of left and collided with another car. Seems an odd thing to do. Everybody knows you have to give way to traffic coming from the right on roundabouts.'

'He'd been living in Canada for years and wasn't used to our traffic regulations. It was probably just momentary forgetfulness.' A sudden thought struck Nicola and she exclaimed in distress. 'Did you say he'd got a fractured arm?'

'Yes, but it's the left one, luckily.'

'It's lucky up to a point, but he still won't be able to take up his job. He's a surgeon, you see, and he was going to work with Mr Bradshaw.'

'Yes, I know. The great man came to see him

but it was while he was still muzzy so I don't suppose they had much useful conversation. I expect the job'll be kept open for him under the circumstances, don't you?'

'I hope so,' Nicola said gravely, 'but I can't imagine what he'll do in the meantime.'

'That's *his* problem. I expect he'll solve it somehow, as soon as he's fit enough. Are you coming to see him? He hasn't had any visitors.'

'Me?' Nicola was startled and showed it. 'Concussion patients are generally better without visitors, except close family.'

'According to the notes, his close family is in Canada. I really think you ought to come, Nicky.'

'You're sure he's got over his concussion?'

'Seems to. Anyway, it wouldn't hurt him to see a casual acquaintance like you.'

Had Janet emphasised those two words just a little? Nicola wasn't certain and didn't pursue the matter. 'I'll come on Monday evening,' she decided. 'That will give him another two days to recover.'

They spent an enjoyable morning wandering round the shops, though neither of them bought anything. After that Nicola was faced with the necessity of occupying herself during the weekend. Recently she had spent all her spare time with Steve. He had been depressed because he was on the dole and his ego had needed constant bolstering. At times it had been a little wearisome, she now admitted, but nevertheless the ending of their relationship had left a gap which she did not yet know how to fill.

It was a relief when Monday came and she could go back to work. The surgeries were always extra-busy after a weekend and both doctors had need of her services. She bandaged cuts, took out stitches and helped with difficult children, and then in the afternoon she had a clinic for expectant mothers.

It was Women's Institute night in the village and her mother went off early; consequently Nicola was able to leave for the hospital without any tiresome explanations.

The Debenbridge General Hospital stood on a slight hill. It was a vast conglomeration of buildings and only the centre part—which was the oldest—had any dignity. But Nicola had long ago ceased to look at it critically and it held a firm place in her heart. In spite of her liking for her present job, she sometimes wished she were back there.

This evening, as she entered through the massive swing doors and turned towards the orthopaedic wards, her thoughts were only of the coming visit. It seemed ridiculous to be nervous and yet she certainly was. She was glad to encounter Janet in the short corridor which led to the big old-fashioned ward.

'How is he?'

'Lots better,' Janet said. 'He's in a filthy temper, which is always a good sign.'

'What about his memory?'

'It seems fairly normal but we haven't been asking questions, naturally.' Janet turned away to speak to a couple who had been waiting for her attention.

She was probably in charge tonight, Nicola realised as she went into the ward, and that ought to keep her busy. Although she was glad to have been brought up to date before seeing Chris, she didn't want to have to deal with her friend's curiosity.

Detaining a young student nurse, she asked where his bed was.

'Half-way down on the right.' The girl looked at her with interest and then hurried on her way.

The ward was so full of visitors that it was impossible to see far ahead. There were at least two people at every bed and the atmosphere was cheerful and even noisy, which was not unusual in an orthopaedic ward where a lot of the patients were young and often feeling quite well.

Threading her way slowly, Nicola reached the half-way mark without seeing anyone not fully occupied with visitors. And then she suddenly came on a patient who was quite alone, and she knew she had reached her objective.

But he looked so different. Fading bruises round his eyes and a long, stitched cut across one side of his forehead made him appear gaunt and ill, and slightly hollow cheeks added to the effect. He was leaning back against a heap of pillows, one arm in plaster and the other hand listlessly turning the pages of a magazine. Only his hair was exactly as Nicola remembered it—thick, tawny and a little unkempt.

She stood hesitating at the foot of the bed and he looked up and saw her. They stared at each other for what seemed a very long time and then she found her voice.

'I was so terribly sorry to hear about your accident. I—I thought perhaps you might be a bit short on visitors and so I came to see you.'

His reply came with the abruptness and force of a pistol shot, startling her so much that she stood for a moment totally stricken.

'What the hell for? I don't know you, do I?'

CHAPTER FOUR

SHE OUGHT to have been prepared for it, of course, but somehow it had never occurred to Nicola that Chris might not remember her. They had, after all, spent three whole days together—and just before the accident, too.

'I'm sorry—' she began.

'What are you apologising for? You may as well stay a few minutes and tell me why I'm supposed to know you.' He flung down the magazine and looked at her expectantly.

He was the one who should have been apologetic, Nicola thought bitterly. She was still sore after the rudeness of his greeting and would have liked nothing better than to go away and leave him to stew in his own bad temper. But with an effort she pulled herself together and spoke quietly and coolly.

'My name is Nicola Craven and we met last weekend at—at Sandbeach.' She paused, but the names seemed to mean nothing to him. He was staring at her as blankly as ever. 'I expect your concussion hasn't quite cleared up,' she suggested. 'Please don't try to remember. It wouldn't be good for you.'

'How do you know that?' he demanded.

'I'm a nurse.'

'I see.' Chris frowned and brushed his hand across his forehead. 'Well, I don't recall ever having heard of you, Nicola, and I've no intention of pretending anything different. As a matter of fact, the whole of last weekend seems to have been wiped from my mind. I know I was on holiday abroad and I remember coming back to this country to take up my job with Mr Bradshaw, but I can't even remember the accident.'

Nicola was still standing at the foot of the bed but now she moved hesitantly towards the chair at his side. 'Shall I stay for a little while?' she asked. 'Or don't you want to be bothered?'

'It's up to you.' His tone could scarcely have been more indifferent.

'I don't want to tire you.'

'For God's sake—I'm not an invalid! I just happen to have a few fractures, that's all. Sit down and stop handling me so flaming gently.'

'Okay. I'll be brutal and talk about the future.' She sat down promptly. 'What did Mr Bradshaw say to you? Is he keeping the job open?'

Chris turned his head and stared at her. 'How did you know he'd been to see me? Who told you?'

'Janet did—that is, Staff Nurse Martin. She works in this ward.'

'Martin?' He frowned again and winced as though it hurt him. 'The pretty blonde?' And when she nodded he asked, 'I suppose you work in this hospital too?'

'Not now.' She explained her job in her uncle's

practice and Chris listened with his eyes half closed. At least, she supposed he was listening but she couldn't be sure until he commented at the end,

'If it's a big group practice I imagine there's plenty for you to do.'

'It isn't actually, though I'm still kept busy. There's only my uncle and his partner. They really ought to find another doctor to help out and Dr Featherstone would be all in favour of it, but Uncle won't give in.'

This time Chris had nothing to say and Nicola realised that she had stayed long enough. But he still hadn't answered her question about his future at Debenbridge General and she badly wanted to know what the heart specialist had decided.

'Have they told you how long it will be before you can tackle surgery?' she asked tentatively.

His lips twisted into a wry grimace. 'About three months, Bradshaw thinks. I don't know how the hell I'm going to fill up all that time, but I suppose something will turn up.'

'He *is* keeping the job for you, though?'

'Yes, of course. I told you, didn't I?' he said irritably.

Nicola did not disillusion him, realising that it was still difficult for him to keep his mind in proper order. It was time to say goodbye and she did it quickly and casually. As she walked back down the ward she wondered whether they would ever meet again.

It seemed unlikely and yet exactly the same query had been in her mind just a week ago. She had half hoped for another meeting then, she now admitted, but no doubt it was only because she was grateful to him for helping her through a difficult patch. It was impossible to pretend that she had been any comfort to him in his present circumstances.

'Are you coming again?' Janet called as she passed the office door.

Nicola paused. 'I don't think so. Chris wasn't particularly pleased to see me.'

'I warned you he was in a filthy mood just now. It's part of his convalescence.'

'Yes, of course.' Nicola hesitated and then added with some reluctance, 'You can let me know if you think there's any point in my turning up again.'

'I'll give you a ring,' Janet promised.

But she did not do so and Nicola was obliged to conclude that her visit to Chris had been as big a mistake as she had thought at the time. Yet she couldn't entirely erase his image from her mind. She had only to close her eyes and she could see him as he lay on the beach at her side—magnificent in his male health and strength, clear-skinned, good-looking and very sure of himself.

At the end of two weeks she phoned Janet with the intention of fixing up another coffee rendez-vous.

'Sorry—I'm on duty all the weekend and I start my holiday the following week. We'll have to arrange something when I get back,' Janet said.

'How's Chris?' Nicola forced herself to ask.

'Discharged yesterday. He's gone to the convalescent home at Riverside Park.'

'Did he get his memory back completely?'

The question seemed to surprise Janet. 'As far as I know. He's seemed perfectly normal for some time, though still fuming at the interruption in his career. He's dead keen on surgery, as I expect you've gathered, and I reckon he'll go far. Probably be a consultant himself before he's thirty-five.'

So that was that, Nicola reflected when the conversation had ended. Now she really could write off that weekend as something that had better be forgotten. But even as she came to that conclusion, something Chris had said flashed into her mind. 'It really seems as though fate is determined to fling us together.'

It hadn't been fate last time, though, but her own misguided visit to him in hospital. And how much she still regretted it!

During the next two weeks she flung herself into her job with even more than her usual dedication, doing all she could to ease the path of the overworked doctors. Shortly after her conversation with Janet there was an outbreak of summer flu in Moresham, which added considerably to the work-load.

Perhaps it was the proverbial last straw. Whatever the reason, Dr Hardwick called her into his consulting room one evening, just before starting his calls, and announced that he had some surprising news for her.

'Yes?' She looked at him expectantly, noting his ashen look of fatigue. 'What is it, Uncle?'

'Peter Featherstone and I have reached a great decision. I can't say I'm exactly in favour of it, but there comes a point beyond which one can't push oneself any further.'

What on earth was he on about? Nicola waited impatiently and wished he would get on with it.

'The way things are at the moment, neither of us will have a chance of getting away on holiday,' Dr Hardwick continued. 'And we both need one extremely badly. Accordingly, we have decided to try the experiment of taking an assistant.'

'Oh, I *am* glad! I'm sure you won't regret it.'

'That remains to be seen,' he said rather grimly. 'I know nothing about the young man, except what he's told me himself, but he's not lacking in self-confidence—which may or may not be a good thing. He's got one disadvantage, unfortunately, but I expect we can get round it.'

'What's that?' Nicola asked curiously.

'His left arm is in plaster, due to a motor accident. I must admit it seems to inconvenience him very little and he has the use of his fingers, but if he has to visit any distant patients I'm afraid he'll require you to drive him.'

For a moment Nicola was speechless. It didn't *have* to be Chris, but surely there couldn't be much doubt about it? Trying hard to speak naturally and making a poor job of it, she asked his name.

'Dr Christopher Felgate.' Her uncle seemed to have noticed nothing odd about her manner. 'Goodness knows how he heard about our needing help. He said rather vaguely it was "on the grapevine" and I suppose these things get around. Anyway, he turned up at my private house last evening and it was all fixed up very quickly.'

Somehow Nicola had managed to pull herself together. 'When does he start, Uncle?' she asked.

'Next Monday. Fortunately we have plenty of space here and Felgate can have his own consulting room—that one across the hall which I sometimes use for examinations. See that he has everything he needs, and you'd better come downstairs early and be ready to show him round.'

'Yes, Uncle,' she said meekly, and thankfully escaped. Upstairs, she was so quiet for a while that her mother enquired if she was tired.

'Not particularly. I was thinking, that's all.' Nicola took a deep breath. 'Uncle had some astonishing news.'

She was not surprised at Alison's reaction when she was put in the picture. 'Thank goodness James has seen sense at last.'

On Monday morning Nicola went downstairs early, as instructed. She spent some time moving things around. The examination couch could stay where it was and she managed to find an unused table in the storeroom. It didn't look very imposing but it would have to do. She took two chairs out of the waiting room which, fortunately, was well supplied, and also one of the numerous indoor plants which she put on the window sill of the new consulting room.

Chris probably wouldn't notice it, but at least she had done her best for him. Very correct in her bright blue uniform dress and red belt, she stood talking to Mrs Robson while she waited for him to arrive.

'It seems an awful pity the new doctor can't drive,' the woman said. 'Whoever heard of a doctor not having a car?' Seeing Nicola's expression she added hastily, 'I know it wouldn't be much good to him just now, not with one arm in plaster but—' She broke off and stared in alarm towards the big window overlooking the road as a loud metallic crash shook the glass. 'Whatever's that?'

'Sounded like an accident.' Nicola leapt to the window and stared out in horror to where a coach had slewed across the road, one side badly dented and broken glass scattered about. There were the white faces of children beyond the shattered windows and people were running from the houses all around.

'It's the school bus!' Mrs Robson had joined her.

Nicola plunged towards the hall and erupted

from the front door. As she shot out of the drive entrance she almost fell over a motor cycle lying on its side on the path. The rider, a black leather-clad figure, was lying very still a few yards away.

'Lucky for him he was thrown clear,' said a middle-aged man, looking down at him with no visible sign of concern. 'More than he deserved, if you ask me—came out of that lane like a bat out of hell, slap into the bus. Driver didn't have a chance.'

Unable to share his attitude, Nicola went down on her knees and felt for a pulse. It was beating quite strongly and she was about to make a further examination when her informant, together with several other people who had joined the little group, was thrust aside in a peremptory manner.

'Stand back!' Chris ordered in a loud voice and with such authority that the onlookers automatically obeyed. He glanced at Nicola. 'Have you phoned for an ambulance?'

'There hasn't been time,' she protested.

'Then do it now. This chap will probably need to be taken to Casualty and some of the kids in the coach as well, very likely. You'd better take a look at them when you come back.'

Noting that the motor cyclist's eyes were now open, Nicola jumped up and hurried back towards the house. In the doorway she met Mrs Robson.

'I've rung the hospital,' the receptionist told her. 'Is there anything I can do to help?'

'I think there soon will be. I'm going to bring all the children who aren't much hurt in here. We can't leave them sitting in the coach.'

Most of the occupants were badly frightened, tears and blood from cuts streaming down their faces, but some of them appeared to be thoroughly enjoying the excitement. The driver was still in his seat and apparently unhurt, though dazed and shocked. Seeing Nicola's uniform he spoke over his shoulder to a young teacher bleeding from a cut on the head.

'Thank God, here's someone who knows what she's doing! Don't you upset yourself no more, miss—the nurse'll soon sort things out for you.'

'I've been trying to find out which of them need hospital treatment.' The girl mopped at her face with a blood-stained handkerchief. 'But they keep getting mixed up again.'

'Leave it to me,' Nicola said cheerfully. 'I'll manage it somehow.'

Suddenly inspired, she seized a stolid-looking child who was surveying the scene with comparative calm. She was neither bleeding nor tearful and seemed willing to help.

'You see that big house over there, the one with the door standing open? Well, I want you to take the unhurt children two or three at a time across the road and into the hall. You'll find somebody there.'

'Okay.' The girl clutched at two smaller children next to her. 'I'll take Gary and Janice first, miss. There's nothing the matter with them 'cept they feel sick.'

A policeman had appeared and was controlling the small amount of traffic. He made no attempt to interfere with Nicola's plan and the operation went with surprising smoothness. She was vaguely aware that an ambulance had arrived but she was so intent on her job that a voice from the door startled her.

'How many in here need medical attention, Nurse?'

'About fifteen,' Nicola told the ambulance man, 'but some of them we could deal with ourselves. They've got very minor cuts.'

Agreeing at once, he picked up a little girl who was crying hysterically and handed her down to his colleague standing in the road. In a short time the coach was empty.

'You'd better come in too,' Nicola said to the driver. 'I expect you could do with a cup of tea.'

'Thanks very much, miss. I'd be glad of one. It wasn't my fault, you know—that young idiot never looked right nor left, though you'd think a bus was big enough to be seen.' He looked about him as they crossed the road. 'What happened to him? Was he badly hurt, d'you know?'

'I've no idea. You'll have to ask the doctor.'

Chris was in the hall, marshalling a line of children who were waiting to wash. He hailed Nicola with relief.

'This is more your job than mine, and you'll

have to plaster their cuts too. I can't manage it with one hand and I don't know where you keep things either.'

'I was going to show you round before surgery started, but the accident put paid to that.'

Mrs Robson was presiding over a tea tray and she handed a cup to the driver who received it gratefully. As he stood sipping it Nicola remembered his anxiety over the motor cyclist and put the question for him.

'He was temporarily knocked out,' Chris said, 'but there didn't seem to be any fractures, as far as I could tell. I brought him in for a while, until the ambulance arrived, and then packed him off for X-ray.' He frowned and said in a disgusted tone, 'Cheeky young devil!'

'Why do you say that?' she asked curiously.

'I took my eyes off him for a minute or two and he disappeared. I found him exploring the place and he said he was looking for the toilet. It's right there in the hall with a label on the door.'

'Maybe he couldn't read,' the driver said sourly. He gave a sudden exclamation. 'The police! They'll be wanting to take a statement.'

'They'll know where to find you and there's no reason why they shouldn't take it in here. Go and sit down over there and finish your tea in comfort.'

'Come and have a cuppa yourself, Doctor,' Mrs Robson put it. 'I reckon you could do with it. You mustn't expect this excitement every morning,' she went on chattily, and then broke off abruptly as the front door opened.

Dr Hardwick, immaculately dressed as usual, stepped inside and halted to stare round in amazement. 'What the devil's going on?' he demanded.

The black and white tiles were littered with odd items of clothing, lunch-boxes, polythene bags in various bright colours and innumerable other objects belonging to the children. A babel of childish voices came from the patients' toilet, interspersed with shrieks of anguish as the hot water discovered several small cuts.

'There's been an accident—' Nicola began, but was impatiently interrupted.

'I know that—the coach is still outside. I assume it was a school party.' He glanced in disgust round the untidy hall. 'But why are these children here? This is a doctor's surgery, not a casualty department.'

'These aren't casualties,' Chris explained. 'Most of them aren't hurt at all.'

'How can you be sure of that? They should have gone to hospital for a check-up with the others. They should *not* have been brought in to disturb my patients and disrupt my morning. What do you suppose we're going to do with them now?'

Behind him the door opened again and a policeman looked in. 'Where's that driver?' he asked.

The man half rose and the officer—who was young and a stranger in the neighbourhood—

crossed the hall to him, giving Dr Hardwick a casual nod in passing.

'This is really too much!' James Hardwick exploded. 'Who gave you permission to do your interviewing on these premises?'

The driver broke in hastily. 'The doctor said it would be all right—'

'*What* doctor?'

Nicola glanced apprehensively at Chris. If he should lose his temper it would be a disastrous start to his new job.

Fortunately he seemed to have himself well under control and he said casually, 'He's referring to me. I was the only doctor here at the time and somebody had to take charge. I didn't think you'd mind the hall being made use of under the circumstances.'

Sensing that her uncle was about to make it plain that he minded very much indeed, Nicola broke in hastily.

'I can soon get the place tidy again and I'm sure the patients won't object to a little confusion. People are usually very sympathetic where children are concerned.'

'And in the meantime, if I need your services I suppose I must manage without them.' With another disgusted stare round the hall, her uncle stalked into his consulting room.

Nicola sighed and was about to return to her charges when she found Chris at her side. To her dismay he was looking as angry as Dr Hardwick had done.

'Let's get this straight once and for all.' His voice was very quiet but it vibrated with indignation. 'I do not—repeat *not*—need your protection when dealing with my employers. I'm perfectly able to stand up for myself, so in future kindly keep your motherly instincts under control.' His tone changed and he was brisk and businesslike. 'Do I rate a consulting room of my own or is that too much to expect?'

'It's over here.' Nicola flung open the door so fiercely that it crashed back against the wall. 'Sorry I haven't got time to show you round properly just now.'

But as she left him alone her anger died as quickly as it had been born and depression took its place. If it was going to be like this every day she might find herself wishing that Chris had never even heard of Drs Hardwick and Featherstone.

Common sense soon reasserted itself. There wouldn't be an accident outside every day, and Chris would rapidly find his own niche in the practice and settle into it. In fact, by the end of that first Monday he already seemed thoroughly at home. And when he rang up to ask Nicola to join him for a celebration drink at the pub she had no hesitation in accepting.

CHAPTER FIVE

THE NEW INN was old and rather dark, with a centuries-old smell of beer and tobacco. It was less than five minutes' walk away from the doctor's house and it did not even occur to Nicola to use her car.

There was no sign of Chris in the bar, but he joined her almost at once with a casual apology.

'Your uncle gave me one or two calls to make after supper and tramping around took quite a bit of time.' He grinned a little ruefully. 'I reckon I ought to be fighting fit when I've finished this job.'

'He knows it's only temporary, I suppose?' Nicola asked.

'What do you take me for? I told him all the facts, naturally, and I think he was rather glad that there'd be a way out for him if having an assistant didn't work out. If it *does* work—and I don't see any reason why not—he'll look round for somebody more permanent and take him on with a view to partnership.'

He took a long thirsty drink of beer and Nicola sipped her lager and lime. As she did so it occurred to her that she knew nothing whatever of Chris's arrangements for providing himself with a roof over his head while he was at Moresham.

'Where are you living?' she asked.

'Here.' He seemed surprised at her ignorance. 'It's a bit primitive but it'll do for the time being. I lost the flat at the hospital, of course, when I had the smash-up.'

'It must be a strange feeling to be homeless.'

'Not particularly. And I don't much care for the image—it makes me sound like a stray dog.'

It didn't suit him, Nicola had to admit, but she didn't dwell on it because she had another question ready.

'What happened to your lovely new car? Was it completely wrecked?'

'It could hardly be expected to survive an encounter with a container lorry.' He gave her an odd sort of look across his glass but made no further comment.

After that they talked about the practice and the neighbourhood and other harmless topics, until Nicola looked at her watch and announced that it was time for her to leave.

'I'll walk along with you,' Chris said.

'Whatever for?' Her astonishment was genuine. 'It's no distance at all.'

'Perhaps not, but I don't want it on my conscience that you got mugged because I wasn't with you,' he told her firmly.

'Mugged? In Moresham?' Nicola laughed outright. 'You have to be joking! It could easily happen in Debenbridge but not *here*.'

'My dear girl, it can happen anywhere, and since it's now dark and the village doesn't run to street lamps, I shall do my duty and escort you home.'

That could have been better put, she reflected wryly, but she made no comment. They set out in silence but Chris soon broke it.

'I've been wondering why you asked about my "lovely new car." Who told you it was new?'

'I expect you did,' she hedged.

'At Sandbeach?'

Janet had said that his memory now seemed normal, but here was proof that it still hadn't completely recovered. Although she could see that from his point of view that must be unsatisfactory, it was impossible for Nicola not to be thankful on her own account.

'Probably at Sandbeach,' she agreed. 'Does it matter?'

'It matters that I can't remember about it. I feel it gives you a considerable advantage over me and I don't care for that at all.'

'You wouldn't, of course,' she said carelessly. 'I should think you'd find it extremely irksome to be at a disadvantage.'

To her astonishment, Chris stopped abruptly, seized her by the shoulders and shook her.

'What's the matter with you? Why do you keep needling me like this?'

'I *don't* keep needling you! I only do it now and then and—and I suppose you just happen to have that effect on me.'

She waited for his explosion of wrath but it didn't come. Instead, his reaction was entirely different. With an angry movement he snatched her to him, forced her head back and pressed his mouth hard on hers. It was certainly not a kiss of love, nor even caused by a temporary sexual urge. Thinking about it afterwards, Nicola could only conclude that it was an instinctive wish to dominate her, to prove that his was the stronger personality.

But at the time she was so deeply shaken that she actually trembled when it was over.

'You shouldn't have done that,' she said when she could speak. 'Why did you?'

'I wanted us to be friends. If we're going to work together it's important.'

'You chose an extraordinary way of starting a friendship. I wouldn't advise you to continue on the same lines.'

She had expected a sharp retort, but instead of that he laughed, quite gently and with genuine amusement.

'At least a guy knows where he stands with you, Nicola. You don't mince words.'

It was only another hundred yards to the doctor's house and they did not speak again until they reached it. As they stopped at the entrance Chris studied the austere Georgian front.

'Seems a nice place. Dr Hardwick told me he used to live here himself. What made him move out?'

'It was after my parents were divorced.' Nicola

stole a glance at his face in the light of the outside lamp, but Chris showed no sign of having heard that before. And they had talked a lot about family relationships during that weekend.

'I don't see the connection,' he said.

'Mum wanted to leave our house in Debenbridge, and Aunt Shirley—that's Mrs Hardwick—was tired of running this big place. So she and my uncle moved to something smaller and more modern, and the first floor here was made into a flat for us. It's useful to have somebody on the premises and so everybody was pleased with the arrangement.'

'Did you mind very much about the divorce?' he asked, an unusually gentle note in his voice.

Nicola's expression hardened. 'Not after I knew my father had gone off with another woman. It was obviously the best thing for Mum, and I like living in Moresham.'

'I'm lucky,' he told her. 'My parents are happily married and so are both my sisters.'

He had mentioned that at Sandbeach.

But again she was careful not to remind him of his amnesia, and they said a quick and entirely casual good night. When she reached the flat Alison looked at her curiously.

'That young man doesn't let the grass grow under his feet!'

'What's that supposed to mean?' Nicola demanded.

'You only met this morning and he's already asked you out for a drink. Fast work, I call that.'

Nicola flushed with annoyance and a certain amount of embarrassment. For a moment she toyed with the idea of admitting that she and Chris knew each other very much better than her mother imagined. But to do so would involve a great deal of explanation, and Alison would certainly be suspicious of that weekend, though she wouldn't actually ask questions.

Since Chris himself had apparently had it wiped completely from his mind, it seemed better for Nicola to forget it as quickly as possible.

And so she said calmly, 'You can call it what you like, Mum, but it was nothing more than a quiet drink to celebrate Chris's first day in the practice. He's living at the local at present and I expect he's found the evenings are a bit boring when he's not working.'

'I hope James will give him plenty to do. The majority of the patients live in Moresham, I believe, so he'll be able to reach most of them on foot.'

During the days that followed both doctors made full use of their new assistant. He had his own round, and occasionally they took him with them when they visited more distant patients so that he should become as familiar as possible with their list.

'Seems a nice chap,' Dr Featherstone said to Nicola. 'Very sure of himself, of course, but that's all to the good. It gives the patients confidence.'

Nicola kept in the background as much as possible, glad that so far there had been no need to use the Mini for Chris's calls. She had not forgotten his scornful voice that first morning when he had accused her of being motherly and so she did not offer him any help unless he actually requested it. These occasions were rare and soon almost everyone ignored the plastered left arm as naturally as he did himself.

Steve had actually enjoyed being mothered, Nicola remembered, looking backwards for a moment. The recollection caused her to think about him briefly and to wonder how he was getting on. With Steve, no news was likely to be good news, but the circumstances of their parting weren't normal and perhaps even he would hesitate to communicate with her.

She dismissed him from her mind and glanced at her watch to see if it was lunch-time. The surgeries were very quiet, with an empty waiting room and the only sound the clicking of Mrs Robson's typewriter. But just as Nicola turned towards the stairs she heard the phone ringing and paused. She'd better wait a minute, just in case it was an emergency.

A moment later the receptionist poked her head out into the hall. 'Nicola! Come and talk to this patient, dear. She's in such a state I can't make out what she's saying.'

She went willingly and lifted the receiver. 'Who is it?' she asked, and immediately an agitated voice broke in on her.

'Mrs Conway—it's my husband! Oh dear, he's in a dreadful state, I don't know what to do—'

'Just try and tell me what's happened, Mrs Conway,' Nicola interrupted. 'Has he got a pain in his chest, for instance?'

'That's it exactly—and he looks terrible. Oh, do please get one of the doctors to him quickly—'

Her mind working like lightning, Nicola turned to Mrs Robson. 'My uncle's ten miles away and Dr Featherstone's busy with that maternity case. I wonder if I can catch Dr Felgate at the pub? He might have called in for some lunch.'

The call was answered by the publican's wife, who seemed to have difficulty in hearing against a background of noise, but eventually Nicola got her message through.

'He's just come in so you're in luck. Hang on a minute and I'll get him.'

And then Chris came on the line, his voice calm and deep and very professional. He listened without interruption and then said briefly, 'I think this is a case for the Mini. I'll expect you in two minutes flat.'

Fortunately the little car was waiting outside and Nicola leapt into the driving seat. She was at the pub well inside the allotted time and found Chris already standing at the entrance to the car park.

'Step on it, Nicola,' he ordered. 'We've got to be quick.'

They sped along the narrow country roads almost in silence. The patient lived in what had once been the lodge to a big estate and fortunately Nicola knew the way well. The imposing iron gates stood wide open and she swept through, drawing up with a flourish before the single-storey house just inside.

'Fifteen minutes,' Chris said, looking at his watch. 'If it was a heart attack it's probably over by now or else—' He did not finish the sentence but Nicola understood his meaning.

The front door opened as they got out of the car and one glance at the face of the woman who stood there told them what they needed to know. Their worst fears had not been realised.

'Robert seems better now,' Mrs Conway said shakily, her pale middle-aged face still showing signs of the ordeal through which she had recently passed. 'I do hope you won't think I shouldn't have bothered you, but I was so frightened. He never had anything like that before. An awful pain in his chest, it was, and seemed to go right down his arm. He couldn't seem to get his breath neither.'

'You were quite right to send for help,' Chris assured her emphatically as they went into the house. 'Where is he?'

'Through here, Doctor.' She opened the door on the right and ushered them into a sitting-room where an elderly man, very ill-looking and with a blue tinge round his lips, sat in a rocking-chair. 'I don't know if he should have gone to bed but he says he feels more comfortable sitting up.'

'That's understandable.' Chris began a careful

examination, handling the patient with great gentleness and kindness.

As Nicola watched, she realised that this case must be just the sort that most interested him. But for the accident he would have been dealing with patients like Mr Conway—and others far more serious—every day.

'I'm going to give you an injection,' he said when he had finished, 'which will stimulate the heart, and I'll leave you some tablets to take regularly.'

'It *was* a heart attack then?' Mrs Conway asked. 'I thought it must be, but I haven't had any experience of that sort of thing. Besides, Robert's always been so fit for all he's ten years older than me.'

'Your husband has had an attack of angina— not, fortunately, a very serious one. But he should come to the hospital for a check-up. I'll get them to send you an appointment and give you a letter to Mr Bradshaw, the heart specialist. In the meantime, see that he has plenty of rest and doesn't do any strenuous work. I take it he's retired?'

'Oh yes—last year. He was gardener up at the house. He only has to look after our own little garden now and I can easily manage that for a bit.' For the first time she seemed to notice his left arm. 'Been in an accident, have you, Doctor?'

'Yes, but I'm mending fast.' He smiled.

'It doesn't seem to make much difference to

your doctoring, anyway.' She led the way into the hall and opened the front door. 'I'm ever so grateful to you for coming so quickly.'

'I'm glad we were able to.' Chris paused on the threshold. 'Try not to worry, Mrs Conway. People with angina can lead a perfectly normal life if they take care of themselves.'

Pursued by further effusive thanks, they left the lodge and got into Nicola's car.

'I believe you enjoyed that,' she ventured as she drove out on to the road.

'It's very wrong of me, but I'm afraid I did. The cases I've been given so far have tended to be very much routine.'

'Do the ordinary jobs bore you so much?'

'Nothing about being a doctor bores me.' Chris pushed the passenger seat back as far as it would go and tried, without success, to stretch out his long legs. 'I didn't think I'd ever be grateful for a ride in a Mini,' he went on, 'but after walking everywhere it's sheer luxury.'

'Tomorrow's your day off, isn't it?' Nicola said. 'You'll be able to put your feet up and have a good rest.'

'Good God!' He turned towards her indignantly. 'I'm not completely decrepit yet! For your information, I'm planning a completely different sort of day. So far I've seen practically nothing of Debenbridge—a place where I expect to be living in the near future—so I thought I'd take a good look round. Is there anything special I ought to see?'

'There's the castle, and if it rains you can go in the museum, or there's a very good sports centre which might appeal to you more.' She broke into a laugh. 'Sorry—I forgot. Your poor feet might make that out of the question.'

'You can leave my feet alone. I wish I'd never mentioned them.' Chris hunched his shoulders and glowered down the road they were following which, for once, was dead straight. But after a moment he added in quite a different and yet strangely casual tone, 'What's supposed to be the best place to eat in Debenbridge?'

'Depends on what sort of meal you want—a proper lunch or bar snacks.'

'I wasn't thinking of lunch.'

Something in his voice had caught Nicola's attention and she glanced sideways at him as she answered. 'You mean you want to end your day out with a slap-up meal somewhere? I should think you might need it after all that sightseeing.'

He ignored the slight sarcasm. 'As a matter of fact I'm taking a girl out to dinner and I'd like it to be at a really good, up-market sort of place. So where do you suggest?'

CHAPTER SIX

IT WAS Nicola's turn to stare straight ahead. The weather was perfect for a drive into the country and she had been enjoying the bright sunshine on the fields of ripening corn. The trees and hedges were still a deep luxuriant green, without any of the dusty look they would acquire towards the end of the summer. The pink and white flowers of the blackberries had still not turned to fruit, and the hips and haws showed no sign of the bright red they would become later.

'I'm waiting,' Chris said patiently, 'for an answer.'

'Sorry. I was thinking.' Nicola pulled herself together. 'If you're taking someone out to dinner, why don't you ask *her* where she'd like to go? She might have a favourite place of her own.'

'That's exactly what I'm doing.'

They were approaching a sharp corner where it was advisable to change gear. Nicola did so, making such a noise about it that she heard Chris grit his teeth.

'Sorry about that! I'm afraid I wasn't concentrating.' She kept her tone deliberately light.

'I'd be obliged,' he said caustically, 'if you'd kindly concentrate when you're driving me. Anyway, why should my invitation have given you such a shock that you needed to take it out on the car? It isn't very flattering.'

Nicola brushed that aside. 'Let me get this right,' she said. 'If you're actually inviting me to have dinner with you, why don't you do it in the normal way instead of taking such a roundabout route?'

'I like to be different. When are you going to answer my original question about the best place for eating?'

'You seem to be assuming that I've accepted the invitation. How do you know I'm free tomorrow evening? Or are you expecting me to cancel any other arrangements I might have made?'

'Have you made any?'

'Well, no, but—' She broke off in slight confusion.

'Then why bother to mention the possibility?'

That didn't seem to need an answer and Nicola gave it none. They were nearly home now; already in the distance she could see the tower of Moresham church and some of the outlying cottages.

'Are you coming or not?' Chris demanded.

'Yes, please,' she told him meekly. 'But I don't know where to suggest. I'm not very well up in that sort of thing.'

Debenbridge was a big place and there were plenty of restaurants to choose from, but Steve had never been able to afford to take her anywhere exciting. Consequently Nicola had little personal knowledge on which to draw. But as she delved into the recesses of her mind she suddenly remembered Janet mentioning a restaurant called the Garden House. One of the doctors at the hospital had taken her there during a brief affair she had had with him.

'It's absolutely super, Nicola,' she had enthused, 'and really lives up to its name. It's all divided up into alcoves and hidden nooks with flowers and greenery, and you get the feeling that you and your escort have got the whole place to yourselves. *Very* romantic!'

Was that the sort of place Chris had in mind?

'If you're looking for something out of the ordinary,' she said doubtfully, 'I've heard that there's a place near the river which is supposed to be rather special.' And she added an edited version of Janet's description.

He raised his eyebrows and grimaced slightly. 'I can't say the name commends it to me, but so long as the food is worthy of the decor I'm prepared to give it a try. You agreeable?'

'Oh yes—er—thanks. I'd like to go very much.' A sudden thought struck Nicola. 'I expect you'll want me to drive?'

'Certainly not. My idea of an evening out does not include being driven by my partner, particularly when she happens to have a Mini. We'll go by taxi.'

And once more Nicola found herself acquiescing with unusual meekness.

*   *   *

The following day Chris told her airily that it was all fixed up and she was to be ready at seven o'clock in two days' time. From that moment, Nicola began to look forward to the evening with quite astonishing enthusiasm.

First she must decide what to wear. Eventually she chose one of the few new dresses she had bought for her trousseau, one which, so far, she had not taken off its hanger. It was in soft shades of pink, which suited her dark hair, and with it she wore a chunky silver necklace and matching earrings. She washed her hair the night before, blow-drying it with great care, and when the time came to dress she gave more attention to her appearance than she had done for months.

Only a few weeks ago she would have hated the thought of wearing that particular dress with anyone but Steve. Now her only concern was that Chris should like it.

'You look very smart,' was her mother's comment.

'Men like a girl to do them credit when they take her out.'

'It's like that, is it?'

Nicola's eyes flashed. 'What's that supposed to mean?'

'Only that you obviously want to please this young man. I don't know when I've seen you look so attractive.'

It wasn't only the clothes but the stars in her eyes, though Nicola was not aware of that. She was glad to have her appearance praised and at the same time annoyed at the words chosen. Did Chris's approval really mean as much to her as her mother had implied?

Finding no answer she was prepared to accept, she shelved the question. Fortunately she heard his ring at the front door just then and, with a quick and casual goodbye to Alison, she ran downstairs.

Immaculate in a dark suit, his hair sleek and gleaming in the evening light, he looked her up and down briefly. 'Quite a transformation,' he said casually.

Nicola glanced at him doubtfully. Did he like the dress or not? It was impossible to be sure and she wanted desperately to know. Against her better judgment, she tried to find out.

'I don't normally go out to dinner in my uniform! My mother seemed to think I looked very dressed up but the Garden House is a smart place—and—well—' She broke off, waiting for him to pay her a compliment.

But Chris apparently didn't recognise his cue.

'I suppose you're one of those men who always like girls to wear blue,' she finished unwisely.

'Only if they happen to be blondes.' He led the way towards an elegant hired car which bore absolutely no resemblance to a taxi.

As Chris sat down in his corner he burst out laughing. 'Stop fishing, Nicola! I know perfectly well what you're trying to make me say! You look nice and I don't like being manipulated. Anyway, I should have thought your mirror would already have answered the question.'

What did he mean by that? Mortified, she stared out of the window and wondered why she had been such a fool as to embark on verbal skirmishing with anyone like Chris. She did not speak again until they had left the village and were speeding towards Debenbridge.

'Don't spoil the evening by sulking,' Chris said softly in her ear.

'I'm not sulking!' Nicola turned on him angrily and found him smiling. Immediately all her irritation vanished and she was once again eagerly anticipating what lay ahead.

The Garden House looked ordinary enough from the front, with the entrance leading into a comfortable bar. Behind this a green-carpeted corridor led to the restaurant itself, which had been made out of a large conservatory. Soft lighting, rampant creepers and flowering pot plants had turned it into a bower of scented coolness in which a number of small tables were almost concealed.

'Looks a bit spidery,' was Chris's comment. 'I hope you're not scared of them?'

'I wouldn't want one dropping into my food, but a few smallish ones don't bother me.'

A waiter conducted them to the end nearest the river, where sliding glass doors stood open, bringing the ripple of water into the restaurant. Tucked into a corner behind a trellis they found their table awaiting them, its yellow mats and napkins matching the candle which burned steadily, protected from draughts by the shade of an old-fashioned brass lamp.

'This is nice.' Nicola slipped into her chair with a sigh of pleasure.

'It's certainly unusual,' Chris admitted. 'I hope the food is as interesting.'

'I've heard it's very good.'

The reputation of the Garden House was accurate. The pâté with which they started was a speciality of the restaurant and deliciously flavoured with herbs. The salmon which followed was perfectly cooked and served with a deceptive simplicity, and after that came strawberries in wine with clotted cream and a cheeseboard which was bewildering in its variety.

'If the coffee's as good,' Chris said, 'then I shall have no hesitation in awarding the management top marks. I wish more places would go in for good cooking rather than pretentiousness and a lot of French and Greek names which most of the clients can't understand.'

Nicola nodded dreamily and sipped the cool delicious hock which had accompanied the meal. Chris had filled her glass several times and the bottle was empty. Having no driving to worry about he had not hesitated to drink his own share and a kind of mellow contentment enveloped them both. They had stopped bickering long ago and had discussed a number of subjects without any real disagreement.

'It's a pity,' he said suddenly, his eyes on the coffee pot as she poured him a second cup.

Nicola was startled. 'What is?'

'That we appear to require something like this to enable us to get on together without trying to score off each other. Ever since I joined the practice we've argued about nearly everything and it gets a bit monotonous after a time.'

Taken aback by the remark, Nicola looked across the table at him without speaking for a moment. They had got on together well enough at Sandbeach, but Chris had still given no sign of remembering anything about it. She felt almost certain that a freak of amnesia had erased it from his mind.

'It must be because you're so bossy and opinionated,' she pointed out gently, a smile in the depths of her eyes.

'*I* am? What utter nonsense!'

They both laughed and Nicola thought with a pang how wonderful it would be if they could always talk to each other like that. Even with Steve she hadn't been able to say the sort of thing she had just said to Chris. He was apt to take a half-laughing criticism far too seriously and complain of hurt feelings.

She didn't want to think of Steve tonight. But even as she pushed the memory of him away, Chris inadvertently brought him back into her mind.

'Tell me about yourself, Nicola.' He leaned across the table, looking intently into her face. 'Do you realise that we work together and yet I scarcely know one single thing about the real you inside the nurse's uniform? What about the men in your life, for instance? There must be some, though I can't believe there's any special one or you wouldn't have come out with me tonight. Some girls might, but not you.'

Nicola caught her breath. As soon as she had herself fully under control she said steadily, 'There aren't any men just now, but there used to be—Steve.'

'Steve,' Chris repeated thoughtfully, and his eyes dropped to his coffee-cup as though he were searching its dark depths for enlightenment.

She said rapidly, 'We were going to be married but he called it off almost at the last minute. I was upset at the time but I don't mind now.' And without waiting for any comment, she went rushing on. 'How about you, Chris? Have you got a girl tucked away in Canada?'

He appeared to be successfully side-tracked for he answered her question at once.

'Tucked away? What a ridiculous expression! I can tell you with absolute truth that there is no girl in the whole of Canada who could make my pulses beat faster.' But as Nicola raised her eyebrows he added sombrely, 'There was once though—a blonde named Sally, another doctor whom I first met at medical school. I came a cropper over her, I regret to say.'

'I can't imagine that happening to you,' Nicola said carefully.

'I shall take good care it doesn't happen again. No girl is going to treat me the way Sally did, that's for sure.' He spoke fiercely, with great intensity, and Nicola could easily understand the hurt it must have been to his pride as well as his heart.

'What exactly did she do?' she asked.

'Made a complete fool of me—strung me along because I was useful as an escort and never said a word about being engaged to a guy in New York. I only found out by chance.'

'You've got over it now?'

'Of course.'

Was that the truth? Nicola couldn't be certain but there was one thing she was quite sure of. Chris still bore the scar of that unfortunate experience, and not until he loved truly and deeply again could he ever be rid of it.

They left the Garden House soon after that and the hired car—by magic it seemed—was waiting for them outside. Throughout the drive back to Moresham they scarcely spoke and the gap between them on the back seat remained unbridged.

'There's a light on in the flat,' Chris commented as they stood together outside the doctor's house. 'Will your mother be waiting up for you?'

Nicola had already noticed it and wondered about it. Alison usually went to bed early when she was alone, but she had the habit of reading until very late. Her room, though, overlooked the garden and this light was on in the living-room.

'She doesn't usually stay up,' she said, 'but it's not really late so perhaps she simply hasn't gone to bed yet.' She looked up at him. 'You'll come in and have some coffee, won't you?'

Chris put out his hand and took hers in a firm grip. 'I don't somehow feel in the mood for drinking more coffee and making polite conversation—do you?'

'I—don't know.'

He laughed softly. 'Come off it, Nicola—you're no more in the mood for it than I am, so stop pretending.' His voice changed. 'It's a lovely night and quite warm. Do you have a garden at the back of the house?'

'A small one—just grass and shrubs.'

'We don't need a lot of space for saying good night.'

Her heart was beating fast but she went with him willingly. They followed a paved path which showed up faintly in the darkness and then felt grass beneath their feet. There was no moon but the starlight revealed a white-painted seat beneath the sheltering branches of a small tree.

'Everything provided,' Chris commented in a satisfied tone.

He sat down and drew Nicola into his arms. And as she felt the hard pressure of his mouth it seemed to her that this was indeed the perfect ending to an evening which had been happier than any she could remember.

He was holding her in a grip of steel and she could feel the pounding of his heart against her

body. She couldn't have moved away if she had
wanted to, but no such wish entered her head.
All she wanted was for it to go on and on until the
passion which had built up in both of them found
some means of release.

How long they remained there, exchanging the
sweet intimate caresses of a man and a woman
who found each other attractive, she had no idea.
But suddenly she was jerked back to full consciousness by the sound of the church clock
striking half-past.

Half-past what? She hadn't a clue, and when
she asked Chris he only murmured inaudibly and
started kissing her again. With an effort she freed
one hand and peered at her watch. Half-past
twelve! It just wasn't possible.

'Chris—I *must* go now.' She started to
struggle.

'Why?' he demanded.

'It's very late.'

'So?' He rubbed his cheek against hers and she
thrilled to its rough touch. 'You don't want to go
in, do you?'

'N-no, but—'

'Then why talk about it?'

'People can't always please themselves.'

'For heaven's sake!' His voice was explosive.
'That's just a load of rubbish, Nicola. You're
grown up, aren't you? You can stay out as late as
you like.'

'No, I can't, not when I know my mother is
sitting up.' She craned her neck upwards. 'Her

bedside lamp isn't on so she must still be in the front of the house, though I can't imagine why.'

'She's probably watching the late night film.'

'She never does, and I'm truly sorry, Chris, but I really must go now. Thank you for a wonderful evening. It's been just perfect—that lovely car and the gorgeous meal and—and everything.'

'Okay, love.' He kissed her lightly and re-leased her. 'Run along in before I change my mind.'

As she left the shelter of his embrace and the night air stirred around her, touching her bare arms with a chilly breath, Nicola shivered. There was no reason for it, except the obvious one that she was no longer sharing the warmth of Chris's body, yet somehow she felt afraid.

The happiness which had come to her that evening had no solid foundation. She was not so naive as to believe that because a man found her attractive to hold in his arms and caress, he was experiencing anything deeper than an ordinary physical need. The warm, tender feeling which had begun to grow in her own heart was very unlikely to be echoed in his.

She climbed the stairs slowly, struggling to adjust to familiar surroundings and the approach of ordinary life. She had nearly reached the top when she heard a door opening and her mother came out on to the landing.

'I thought you were never coming home.'

There was reproach in Alison's voice and

something else as well, something which Nicola couldn't give a name to.

'We got talking and it never occurred to me you'd wait up, Mum. Why on earth did you bother?'

'I didn't have much option. I've got somebody here waiting to see you and, what's more, I've had him for more than three hours.' Alison paused and then added grimly, 'Steve's turned up again.'

CHAPTER SEVEN

'STEVE'S HERE?' Nicola gasped. 'Oh no!'

'I thought it'd be a shock to you,' Alison said.

'What on earth does he want?'

'To see you, of course. Apparently he sees no reason why what happened a few weeks ago should make any difference to the two of you continuing to be friends. The cheek of it!'

'Steve always had plenty of nerve.'

'In some ways. He didn't have enough to go through with the marriage or break it off decently either.'

Nicola sighed and left the top of the stairs reluctantly. 'I suppose I'd better go and speak to him.'

'I hope you'll make it brief. I'm on my way to bed.'

Steve was stretched out in an armchair, his untidy brown head comfortably nestled into one of Alison's best cushions. But when Nicola entered he leapt to his feet and held out his hands.

'It's great to see you again, Nicky love!' he exclaimed.

'What do you want?' she demanded, ignoring the gesture.

'You're horribly abrupt,' he complained, his

greenish-hazel eyes full of the reproach he could so readily assume. 'I thought I'd get a kinder welcome than that.'

'I can't imagine why. I've absolutely no kind feelings towards you, Steve. And after the way you behaved I don't think you've any right to expect me to be different.'

But even as she spoke, Nicola knew she didn't really feel as vindictive towards him as that. He was still the same Steve, whom she had known and been fond of for a long time, the Steve she had once imagined she could happily marry.

It seemed incredible now that she could ever have been such a fool.

'How is your business going?' she asked, edging the conversation away from more personal matters. 'I hope it's prospering?'

He brightened at once. 'It's doing fine! Kevin—that's the bloke who runs it, you know— is pretty good at organisation and figures and all that, and I've always liked doing things with my hands. We're into video now, of course, and that side of the business is really building up. I reckon I've found my right niche at last, Nicky.'

'I'm very glad to hear it,' she said, meaning every word of it. 'Where are you living? Still over the shop?'

'I'm sharing a flat with Kevin and his sister. Nice girl—she reminds me a bit of you—and a smashing cook.'

If he was being so well looked after, Nicola reflected, he shouldn't have such a forlorn appearance. He was very pale and his eyes were shadowed, and he was hunched into a big sweater as though it were winter.

'Shouldn't you be getting back?' she asked. 'I expect you start work early in the morning.'

Steve did not immediately reply. He was looking at her with a half smile which showed a trace of embarrassment, an emotion which was sufficiently rare with him for it to capture Nicola's attention. As she stared at him apprehensively he began to speak.

'The thing is, Nicky, that I've got problems. The old bike's giving trouble and I don't think I could make it to West Codden tonight. The ride here was pretty hairy and once or twice I thought I'd have to get off and push it. I'm sure I can get it going again in daylight but—'

It was obviously her cue to say something and, in growing dismay, she even recognised what it was. But instead of issuing the invitation he was clearly waiting for, she kept silent, her lips firmly pressed together.

Steve tried again. 'If I thought it was safe, I'd struggle back as far as Debenbridge and knock up the family. Mum wouldn't be pleased but she'd find me a bed on the sofa. I can't have my old room because she's given it to my eldest brother. A big family like ours is a bit cramped, you know. We don't have the space you've got here.'

He broke off and gazed at her appealingly. 'Are you receiving me?' he asked wistfully.

'Is your bike really unsafe?' Nicola demanded.

'Of course it is, and I don't feel very fit either. I think I've got a bit of a chill.' Seeing her expression, he added hastily, 'But I shall be okay in the morning.'

'In other words, you want to stay the night.'

'I don't know where else I can sleep,' Steve said pathetically.

Belatedly, Nicola saw it all. The idea of spending the night at the flat must have come to him immediately when his motor bike started to show signs of letting him down but, understandably, he had not had the nerve to mention it to her mother. No doubt he believed she—Nicola—was made of less stern stuff. And it was true too, she thought ruefully. She couldn't possibly harden her heart and turn him out.

Yet she hated the thought of offering him the bed in which they had been going to sleep together. The mere sight of Steve in that room, so carefully decorated and made attractive by her own efforts, would be painful to her.

Suddenly she was too tired to fight any more. It had been an evening of great emotional upheaval and she was exhausted.

'Wait here and I'll make the bed ready,' she told him in a resigned tone which gave no clue to her real feelings.

Going grimly about her task of locating double sheets in the airing cupboard, she was so torn by conflicting passions that she longed to sit down and surrender to tears. Memories of the past rose up to confront her; of Steve in a sweet and loving mood, and happy days they had spent together before the stern gateway of marriage had cast its dark shadow over their path.

Her vision blurred as she tucked in sheets and blankets, and into her mind there flashed an echo of their argument about duvets. She had wanted to buy one for their bed but Steve had opposed it.

'Just being married will be a big enough change without having to cope with a duvet as well,' he had protested.

Nicola had laughed at the absurdity, but she now realised that he had given her a hint of his true feelings, if only she had had the wit to see it. Lost in thought, almost totally absorbed by the intrusive past, she did not hear the door open behind her. But when she felt the pressure of lips on her neck she whirled round with a stifled scream.

'That's not a very nice reaction,' Steve said reproachfully.

'How dare you do that! I can't imagine what made you believe you had the right to—to touch me.' Nicola's eyes flashed.

'Who's talking about rights?' His eyebrows rose. 'I never used to have to ask permission before I kissed you.'

'Everything's different now. You forfeited all that when you stood me up.'

To her dismay, his arms slid round her waist and he drew her close. As she began to struggle he spoke in a low, bitter tone.

'Shall I tell you something, Nicky? There have been quite a number of times when I've regretted what I did. I've missed you so dreadfully. You were around in my life for such a long time and then suddenly you weren't there at all and I knew it was all my own fault.' He hesitated, strangely unsure of himself. 'Would it be too much to ask if we could put the clock back?'

For a moment Nicola was too astonished to speak. The effrontery of it was unbelievable. And as she backed away, consumed by rage, the recollection of how she had felt down there in the garden with Chris swept over her. Her whole body had responded to the rapturous pain of his kisses and the mere thought of reinstating Steve was nauseating to her.

'You've got a nerve!' She flung the words at him furiously. 'I would never agree to it—never! I've learnt my lesson where you're concerned and I shan't ever again be able to trust you.'

Steve's eyes widened in dismay. 'I wouldn't have believed you could be so hard, Nicky. I thought you loved me—'

'I imagined I did once, but I think I must have been muddling up a number of other emotions and calling it love. One thing's for sure, though. I don't love you now, Steve. You've got to accept that.'

He was looking sulky, in a way that she remembered only too well, but his voice when he answered was surprisingly firm.

'I'm not going to accept anything of the sort.

I'm sure that when you've recovered completely from what I admit was very bad behaviour on my part, you'll feel differently, given a chance.'

'Given a chance?' she repeated. 'What's that supposed to mean?'

'Seeing each other as frequently as possible. West Codden isn't all that far away, and when I get the bike into good working order—' He sat down rather abruptly on the edge of the bed.

On the verge of an explosive retort, Nicola looked at him with a professional eye and decided that he really didn't seem at all fit.

'You'd better get to bed,' she said curtly. 'We've talked far too long already.'

His long, light brown lashes lifted and she saw a flash of mischief. 'I wish I could persuade you to stay here with me, Nicky—it would make such a difference to us both. I wouldn't feel so shivery and you—'

'I've given you more blankets than you should need on a summer night, so stop trying to make me feel sorry for you. How early do you want to be called in the morning?'

'There's no great rush.' He yawned. 'Any time that suits you.'

Outside on the landing, Nicola hesitated, glancing at her mother's door. But there was no line of light round it and she concluded that Alison had given up and fallen asleep. Relieved that she needn't enter into explanations tonight, Nicola retreated to her own room where, to her later astonishment, she slipped almost instantly into a deep sleep.

Her mother brought her a cup of tea as usual. 'What time did that tiresome boy go last night?' she demanded.

Nicola dragged herself reluctantly back to consciousness. 'Steve? He didn't.'

'Didn't go?' Alison stared at her. 'I don't understand.'

'He's in the spare room.' With an effort Nicola forced her half-asleep mind to produce an account which didn't show the visitor up in too bad a light.

But Alison was not deceived. 'It's what he intended all along,' she said angrily. Pulling her dressing-gown more tightly round her thin figure she marched to the door. 'I shan't take *him* a cup of tea, and as soon as he puts in an appearance I shall tell him to get out. The cheek of it—coming here on a faulty motor bike and then foisting himself on us.'

'Don't be too hard on him, Mum,' Nicola begged, sitting up in bed. 'I don't think he's feeling quite as fit as he usually does.'

'Serve him right!' The door banged.

They breakfasted almost in silence, but when they had both finished and there was no sign of Steve, Nicola knew she would have to do something about it.

'He'll be terribly late getting to the shop, even if his bike behaves itself,' she worried. 'I think I'll take him in a mug of coffee—he always preferred that to tea—and then perhaps he'll get moving.'

Alison pursed up her lips but made no comment. When Nicola tapped on the door of the spare room there was silence inside so she turned the handle and went in.

'It's eight o'clock, Steve—do wake up.'

The only reply was a grunt from the hunched figure in the bed, and she crossed the room to draw the curtains back and let in some light. Immediately there was a loud protest and Steve put his hands over his eyes.

'Do you have to do that? I've got one hell of a headache.'

'I'm sorry, but how was I to know?' She half drew the curtains again. 'Would you like some paracetamol?'

'If you think it will do any good. I feel bloody awful all over, as a matter of fact.' He peered at her over the edge of the bedclothes. 'I can't possibly get up, Nicky, I'm much too ill. You'll have to ring up the shop and explain to Kevin that he must manage on his own today.'

'What do you think is the matter with you?' Nicola exclaimed in dismay.

'How should I know? You're supposed to be the medical expert around here.'

'I didn't think you looked any too good last night. Perhaps you've got a dose of summer flu. There's a lot of it about.'

'Could be. Does it last long?'

'Oh no—only a day or two.' Nicola hesitated, thinking of her mother's wrath, and then continued with what clearly had to be said. 'You'd better stay in bed today and we'll see how you are tomorrow.'

'Okay.' He relaxed with a long sigh, plainly taking it as his right that he should continue to occupy the bed which had so reluctantly been lent him last night. 'Do you think your uncle ought to be asked to take a look at me?'

'I'm sure that's not necessary.' She repressed a smile as she imagined Dr Hardwick's comments should she make such a request. 'I'll bring you a dose now and take your temperature too. I don't suppose you want any breakfast?'

'I think I could manage a bowl of Cornflakes.'

Surprised that he should contemplate eating at all, Nicola went off. As she had expected, her mother had several acid comments to make on the subject of Steve's indisposition but agreed that they would have to put up with him until he felt better.

'He'll have you running in and out fetching and carrying for him all day if you don't look out,' she warned.

'I shan't be here most of the time.' Nicola smiled. 'Perhaps he'll expect you to do it!'

Steve submitted without protest to having his temperature taken and immediately asked what it was.

'Only just above normal,' Nicola said cheerfully. 'Nothing to worry about.'

As she was about to leave him he caught at her hand. 'It's great having you to look after me,

Nicky. Almost as though we'd got married after all.'

Not trusting herself to comment, she hurried out of the room, made the phone call he had requested and went downstairs to begin her day's work. None of the doctors had arrived and it was very quiet on the ground floor. Even the telephone had not started ringing.

She made a quick tour of the consulting rooms to make sure everything was ready for the reception of patients. Chris's looked considerably less bare than it had done originally but, because yesterday had been his day off, it was not untidy and there was nothing for her to do there.

Yesterday . . . It seemed a century ago, and yet the memory of everything that had happened was as vivid in her mind as though it were still going on. Herself and Chris at the restaurant, and then out there in the garden. Herself and Steve upstairs in the flat, and finally Steve in bed complaining of illness.

And suddenly it was all too much for her, so many conflicting emotions, so many demands on her to do this or that, and with a stifled sob she sat down at the desk and let her head rest on her arms.

She must—she simply *must*—have a few moments of peace and quiet before the turmoil of the day began.

'For God's sake!' exclaimed a startled voice from the doorway. 'What's the matter, Nicola?'

She jerked to her feet like a puppet on a string.

'N-nothing—I was just having a rest.'

'At this hour of the morning? Didn't you sleep?'

'Oh yes, but it wasn't the sort of sleep that makes you wake up bright and cheerful.'

What on earth had made her say that? He would immediately want to know the reason.

Chris advanced to the desk and put his hands on it, leaning forward slightly, his eyes intent. 'I slept extremely well myself; in fact, I usually do after a pleasant evening out.' He studied her face, holding her gaze with a mesmerism she couldn't defeat. 'There *is* something the matter,' he said quietly. 'You'd better tell me what it is.'

Nicola sat down again, wrenching her eyes away from that searching stare. She said tautly, 'I got a shock when I went indoors. Steve was there, talking to my mother.'

'Steve,' Chris repeated thoughtfully. 'That's the bloke you were going to marry?'

'Yes.'

He was silent for a moment, perching on the edge of the desk and frowning down at his feet. Then he suddenly looked straight at Nicola again.

'There's nothing very extraordinary about his calling on you, surely? You're very old friends, I believe, and the fact that you imagined you wanted to get married and it turned out a mistake doesn't matter all that much now. He's working quite a distance away, isn't he? You probably won't see him very often.'

'He isn't working anywhere just now,' Nicola told him bleakly. 'He's upstairs in bed, complaining he feels ill.'

'I see.' Both his voice and his expression were totally non-committal. 'I get the impression that you don't quite believe in this sudden illness.'

'Well—' She hesitated, desperately anxious to be fair. 'I don't think he's as bad as he's making out. It may be a touch of flu. He certainly isn't fit.'

Chris stood up with an air of resolution and looked at his watch. 'I've got ten minutes before my first appointment. It won't take that long to discover whether Steve is genuinely ill or not. Besides, I'm rather curious to see this guy who has the power to arouse such strong emotions in you, Nicola.'

'Strong emotions? What do you mean? Steve isn't arousing anything in me just now except irritation.'

'Don't kid yourself,' he told her calmly. 'You're sorry for him and always have been. Your maternal instincts are in full cry, if nothing else is.'

She bit back an indignant retort and led the way into the hall. As they climbed the stairs they could hear Alison clattering dishes in the kitchen with the radio on and she didn't seem to be aware of their arrival.

'Here's Dr Felgate to see you, Steve,' Nicola announced baldly as she opened the door of the spare room.

'Who?' He raised his head languidly from the pillow. 'You're not Dr Hardwick's partner, are you?' he asked in bewilderment.

'Merely the assistant,' Chris said smoothly. 'Let's have a look at your throat.'

As Nicola, trim in her nurse's uniform, stood quietly in the background, she had difficulty in believing it was happening. Who would ever have expected these two men to meet as doctor and patient? The odds against their ever meeting at all must surely have been very great.

'Hm.' Chris was giving nothing away. 'I'd like to listen to your chest now, please.'

Steve struggled up in bed and took off the vest in which he had slept, not having any pyjamas. The effort caused him to take a deep breath and he winced.

'That hurt you?'

'Just a bit.'

Chris adjusted his stethoscope and bent over the patient. He seemed to Nicola to spend a very long time over his examination and she experienced a sudden stab of fear. Surely there couldn't be anything *really* wrong?

CHAPTER EIGHT

CHRIS STRAIGHTENED slowly and looked thought-fully down at Steve, who was now lying back with an air of exhaustion. 'How long have you been feeling ill?' he asked.

'Came on yesterday. I felt very cold when I was riding the bike and I don't usually, not in summer anyway. I thought perhaps I'd got a chill, or maybe flu.'

'Have you had a cold recently?'

'Well, yes. There's been one hanging around for quite a while. I guess I'd sort of got used to it.'

'I'm afraid it's settled in your chest,' Chris said. 'In other words, you've got bronchitis.'

Nicola caught her breath sharply as the full implication of his words hit her like a blow. Bronchitis wasn't serious, provided it didn't become chronic, but it was essential that the patient received adequate nursing care.

'You'll have to stay in bed,' Chris went on, 'and I'll put you on a course of antibiotics. That should clear it up satisfactorily in a few days. You can eat what you fancy, provided it's light, and be sure to drink plenty.' He pushed his stethoscope back into his pocket and turned towards the door. 'I'll see you again in a couple of days' time.'

For a moment Nicola hovered uncertainly and

then she hurried after him. The door closed behind them with a sharp click.

'I would have thought you might have guessed that was rather more than a mere chill,' Chris said as they went downstairs. 'It's a good thing I decided to visit him or you might have turned the poor bloke out and made him ride his motor bike back to West Codden.'

'I hope I would have noticed he wasn't fit enough as soon as he tried to get up,' Nicola protested.

'Perhaps—or, of course, you might have had other things to think about—more personal matters.'

They had reached the hall and she looked at him dubiously, not at all sure what was going through his mind. She would not have expected this sudden concern for Steve's welfare.

'I'm a nurse,' she reminded him. 'I hope I wouldn't let personal matters interfere with medical duty.'

'I hope so too,' he agreed smoothly.

'How long do you think Steve will be ill? His business is doing quite well and he won't want to be away from it any longer than necessary.'

Chris regarded her thoughtfully. 'It depends entirely on how well he's looked after—'

'I would have thought it depended mostly on the antibiotics you're going to dose him with!' Nicola interrupted hotly.

'Those are necessary, of course, but in all these cases nursing is of vital importance. As Steve's physician, I must ask you to remember that.'

Nicola looked at him blankly and found him staring over the top of her head with a deadpan expression on his face. Anyone would think Steve was seriously ill, from the fuss he was making. An overwhelming longing to tell him she didn't want to nurse this unexpected—and most unwelcome—patient, that the very thought of it was repellent to her, came over her.

But there was no time. During their short absence the situation downstairs had changed remarkably. A hum of voices came from the waiting room and Dr Hardwick appeared suddenly in the doorway of his room.

'Where the devil have you two been?' he demanded irritably. 'The waiting room's over-flowing with patients who haven't made appointments.'

As so frequently happened, he had grossly exaggerated the situation. There were only three people who had not telephoned beforehand. One had a badly cut finger, another required a prescription for an elderly relative, and the third had brought a small girl who had a mysterious rash.

Nicola dealt with the first case and Chris attended to the others. To all appearances normality had been restored to the morning which had started so badly.

But beneath the surface calm Nicola carried a hidden heart-break. She had believed that last night was special—and it wasn't. If it had meant anything at all to Chris he wouldn't have behaved so strangely over Steve's illness. It was almost as though he had *wanted* her to nurse the invalid with total dedication.

No sign of her inner turmoil appeared in her manner as she went about her duties, but Dr Hardwick—whose bad temper had continued—made no attempt to hide the fact that he was not in a good mood. It was not until the last patient had gone that she discovered the cause of his ill humour.

'Got called out three times last night,' he grumbled, taking a sip of coffee and grimacing at the taste. 'Why can't we have proper coffee instead of this instant stuff?'

'Because instant coffee is more convenient.' Nicola studied him thoughtfully and decided that he looked tired. 'You don't usually mind all that much about going short on sleep, Uncle. Was there anything special about last night's calls?'

'Only one of them was really necessary, but that's not unusual. People tend to panic at night and a doctor accepts that as an occupational hazard.' Dr Hardwick put down his cup. 'I'll tell you why I feel disgruntled, Nicola. It's because our present situation is ridiculous. Here we are—Peter Featherstone and I—still doing all the night work because our assistant, who's young and healthy, is temporarily unable to drive. An able-bodied chap like that should be capable of taking night calls in his stride.'

'It's not his fault he isn't doing his share,'

Nicola protested. 'And it isn't fair to call him able-bodied with an arm in plaster.'

'It's not only the driving.' He changed direction, determined to finish his grumble. 'Having him living at the pub is most unsatisfactory, from all points of view. There's only the one phone and I don't suppose the landlord would want it used for night calls, in any case.' He finished his coffee and stood up. 'I'm afraid the problem is insoluble.'

Privately agreeing with him, Nicola considered it more diplomatic to say nothing. He would soon recover from his black mood and soldier on as usual.

The waiting room was full again and the babble of conversation even louder than normal as a dozen or more expectant mothers gathered for the ante-natal clinic. Nicola was about to summon the first one when she suddenly remembered the prescription for Steve's medicine, which was still in her pocket. He was probably already considering himself neglected because she hadn't found time to take it upstairs to him.

Like the reception area, the dispensary was staffed by part-timers. It was situated in what had once been the kitchen and was always busy, since the villagers thoroughly appreciated their luck in not having to go into Debenbridge to get their prescriptions made up.

'Lunch-time do, Nicola?' Sue Beyton, a sandy-haired girl in a white overall, asked briskly. 'We're very rushed this morning.'

'It'll have to do.'

As she took the piece of paper Sue glanced casually at the name and her eyebrows rose. 'Steve Paynton? Surely that's—'

'Yes,' Nicola said briefly.

'Is it all on again then? Oh, I *am* glad—'

'No, it's not! I'll come back for the medicine at lunch-time.' Nicola plunged for the door and just managed not to slam it behind her.

Fuming, she hurried to the room where she conducted her clinics, but the mothers-to-be soon took her mind off the problem of Steve. Some were expecting babies for the first time and others had toddlers with them. Nicola worked her way steadily through the list until there were only two left. They were all straightforward this morning and she did not have to advise any of them to make an appointment to see one of the doctors. The last but one was dealt with as expeditiously as the others and departed cheerfully.

'Come in now, Mrs Riley,' Nicola said into the waiting room.

There was no reply and no sound of movement. Surprised, she looked in and found the room empty.

It was so unusual for a patient to disappear that Nicola was a little disconcerted. Finding that no message had been left with the receptionist, she found her concern growing. Mrs Riley had sat silently in a corner, she remembered, and had not appeared to join in the general conversation.

She had clutched her five-month-old baby and stared into space, detached from everything and everybody.

It was her first visit to the clinic in connection with what was presumably a new pregnancy. So why hadn't she waited?

Nicola had several calls to make that afternoon but there would be time for another. Taking out her notebook and pen she added Mrs Riley's name to the list. She would make a casual, friendly visit and perhaps find out what was wrong, if anything.

In the meantime, Steve must be feeling neglected. She collected his medicine and went reluctantly upstairs to lunch. Her mother, who worked flexible hours at the Debenbridge library, was not on duty until the afternoon, and she found her in the kitchen.

'Whoever would have thought it?' Alison's voice was a mixture of incredulity and disgust.

'Thought what?' Nicola asked absently, searching for a small glass.

'That we'd ever have Steve here in that room that was meant for both of you. Do you think he's really got flu?'

'Chris looked in to see him while you were busy earlier this morning and he says it isn't flu.' Nicola took a deep breath. 'It's bronchitis.'

'*What?*'

'Afraid so, Mum. He'll be here for a few days.'

'Oh God—I don't think I can bear it!' Alison picked up a knife and began to slice a cucumber

with unnecessary viciousness. 'I suppose you'll
have to nurse him.'

'It looks like it,' Nicola said briefly, thinking of
Chris's insistence.

Steve appeared to be asleep but he opened his
eyes so quickly that she suspected he had only
closed them when he heard her at the door.

'How're you feeling?' she asked.

'Awful. My chest hurts and I'm all bunged up.
Is that my medicine? You took your time about
bringing it.'

'It wasn't ready until lunch-time.' She admin-
istered a dose. 'Do you want anything to eat?'

'Of course I do. I'm rather hungry, actually.
What were you thinking of giving me?'

'I hadn't thought at all, I'm afraid. How about
a poached egg?'

Steve did not greet the suggestion with any
enthusiasm. 'I'd like something a bit more substantial,' he said wistfully. 'I missed my meal last
evening.'

In the end she brought him a small helping of
the cold meat and salad she and her mother were
having. Alison tightened her lips when she saw
the tray being prepared but refrained from
comment.

'Try and get some sleep this afternoon,' Nicola
advised. 'I'll pop in again when the next dose is
due.'

Steve was not really listening. He was gazing at
her with an expression on his face which filled her
with foreboding.

'I've been thinking a lot while I've been lying here,' he announced, 'and it seems to me that I've been all sorts of a fool. You remember what I said about putting the clock back?'

Nicola's eyes flashed. 'I told you then what I thought of the idea. I don't want to discuss it any more.'

'Don't be like that, Nicky,' he pleaded. 'I'm feeling so ill that I can't cope with you being unkind to me—specially as seeing you again has brought back all the happy memories I'd temporarily forgotten.'

'I'm *not* being unkind—just realistic, that's all. 'It's only because you're not in your normal state of health that you're getting sentimental over the past. Once you're back at work you'll forget all about me again.'

'I'll never forget you,' he insisted. 'You're part of my life—always have been.'

Nicola looked down at him despairingly as her treacherous heart responded to his plea for sympathy and forgiveness. She knew that he believed every word of what he was saying—at the moment of saying it. Perhaps he might even continue to believe it when he got back to West Codden. And perhaps not.

'I'm sure we shall always be friends.' She hesitated and then went on briskly, 'But it's too late for anything else. Can't you see that?'

'It's never too late for love,' Steve said obstinately.

Nicola sighed. 'If you don't stop talking you'll

probably send your temperature up.' She forced herself to speak sharply. 'Do try and get some sleep.'

It was a relief to leave the flat and start out on her calls, and because it was convenient to do so she went first to Mrs Riley's house.

She lived in one of the new estates in a so-called 'town house' and opened the door at Nicola's second ring, her baby in her arms. The child looked well, though slightly overweight, but it was at once apparent that there was something wrong with the mother.

'Hello, Mrs Riley.' Nicola produced a friendly smile and came straight to the point. 'What happened this morning? One moment you were in the waiting room and the next you'd vanished. I thought I'd better check up.'

Mrs Riley hesitated, her colourless face half hidden by lank fair hair. The dark roots were very much on view, Nicola noted, and that was a bad sign. This young woman was usually very conscious of her appearance.

'You'd better come in.' The invitation was grudging and delivered without the slightest sign of animation.

Nicola stepped into the hall. She tickled the baby's double chin and was rewarded with an enchanting toothless smile. 'Gary looks absolutely blooming,' she commented.

'He's doing fine.' The woebegone face brightened momentarily. 'I wish I could say the same for myself.'

'What's the matter then?'

'I'm pregnant again, that's what's the matter—and it was never meant. I didn't hardly know how to bear it this morning with all those other mums so cheerful and pleased with themselves. It fair made me sick to listen to them and suddenly I couldn't stand it any longer, so I got up and went home.'

'Let's sit down.' Nicola led the way into the front room. 'Are you sure about this pregnancy, Mrs Riley? You haven't brought us a specimen.'

'Of course I'm sure. I feel just the same as I did with Gary, and God knows that was something I never wanted to go through again.' She looked down at the child and her expression softened. 'I'll just put him down for his sleep and be right back. There's a lot I want to say to you.'

The room was smartly furnished in a conventional sort of way, with draped net curtains and a big vase of pampas grass. When Mrs Riley returned she perched on the edge of a chair, her face the same colour as the creamy Dralon, and continued as though there had been no interruption.

'My husband doesn't want another baby. He says we can't afford it and he's not putting up with me being the way I was before, not at any price. *And* he says it's all my fault because I was careless.'

She paused and then looked straight at Nicola. 'He wants me to get rid of it, Nurse. That was really why I came this morning and waited till the end.'

Perhaps she should have expected it, but the fact remained that she hadn't and Nicola knew that her surprise and shock was showing in her face.

She spoke more sharply than she had intended. 'You shouldn't have come to the clinic. There's nothing I can do for you.'

'You can put in a word for me, can't you? Say you think I should have an abortion for health reasons?' Mrs Riley leaned forward eagerly.

Nicola shook her head. 'It's not my job at all, and I really don't think you stand much chance of a termination. The reasons you've given me just aren't good enough.'

To her dismay the woman burst into tears. 'I never thought you'd be so hard-hearted—you ought to try being pregnant yourself and then perhaps you'd be more sympathetic!'

'I'm not unsympathetic—really I'm not. I'm only being practical and telling you what's likely to happen. But you don't have to take my word for it. You should make an appointment with a doctor and get your husband to come with you.'

Receiving no reply, Nicola went on gently, 'I'm sure you could do with a cup of tea, Mrs Riley. Do you mind if I go into the kitchen and make some for us both?'

'You'll keep out of my kitchen!' There was venom in the angry voice. 'And you can get out of my house too—you and your daft ideas. Go on—make yourself scarce!'

Nicola hesitated but, distressed by a stare of considerable vindictiveness from the tear-drowned eyes, she reluctantly stood up. 'Please, Mrs Riley, let's talk about it for a little longer,' she begged. 'We can't leave things like this—'

'Oh yes, we can! You can't make me change my mind and it's no good trying, so get out!'

It was useless to argue, that was very clear, but it was unpleasant to feel that she had done more harm than good, that she had been faced with a difficult situation and failed to rise to it. Thinking about it despondently, Nicola couldn't altogether blame Mrs Riley for the muttered, 'Silly bitch,' which followed her from the room.

And yet what else could she have said? Because of her profession she had been bound to present the conventional viewpoint.

With a sigh she reached the parked Mini and felt in her pocket for the key. But before she could fit it into the lock a hand came across from the other side and opened the door for her.

Chris was sitting there.

'It was very careless of you to leave the passenger door unlocked,' he said disapprovingly. 'Anyone could have got in.'

'I always keep it locked—'

'So you didn't bother to check?' He shook his head. 'More carelessness, I'm afraid.'

'Don't *you* start!' Nicola slammed her own door, snapped into her seat-belt and started the engine. 'I've been getting it all round today and I've just had a perfectly horrible interview with a patient—and I'm not in the mood for being told off by you.'

As they whirled down the road she sensed that he was looking at her, but he did not immediately reply. It was not until they had turned the corner that he enquired politely where they were going.

'To my next call, of course. Oh!' She broke off and applied the brake with some vigour. 'I'm sorry—I don't suppose you want to go there at all. Why were you sitting in the car anyway?'

'I saw the Mini and thought you might give me a lift.'

'Where to?'

He mentioned an address on her route, which left her no option but to fall in with his suggestion. As they proceeded at a reduced pace he asked her casually if she wanted to talk about the 'horrible interview' to which she had referred.

'It sometimes helps,' he said, 'to get another point of view.'

To her surprise, Nicola suddenly discovered she wanted to tell him all about it and she did so at once. 'I know I handled it badly,' she confessed, 'but I felt bound to tell Mrs Riley she hadn't much chance of getting her unwanted pregnancy terminated. I'm quite sure neither Uncle James nor Dr Featherstone would agree to it.'

'Nor would I,' Chris said emphatically. 'The health reasons aren't nearly strong enough.'

'There's her mental state, of course.' Nicola paused as they re-entered the main road. 'It's possible she may work herself up into a real tizzy about it. It's not only that they don't want the baby but she had a bad time during nearly the whole of the nine months last time.'

'It won't necessarily happen again. As for not wanting the infant, she'll probably adjust to the idea before long and wonder why she ever asked for a termination.'

His words were comforting and Nicola was grateful. By the time she reached her next visit she had recovered her poise and for the remainder of the afternoon she managed to put both Steve and Chris out of her mind.

CHAPTER NINE

STEVE WAS in bed for the next two days. Nicola nursed him conscientiously and her mother grimly refrained from comment. It was an uncomfortable and unhappy time, with too many emotions simmering beneath the surface.

On the third day Chris announced his intention of paying another visit.

'Your friend ought to be feeling a lot better now. How does he seem?'

Nicola hesitated, trying to disentangle what she suspected to be Steve's enjoyment of being waited on from what his real feelings were with regard to his health.

'He looks pretty well, actually. I think the rest has done him good.'

'It's important in these cases, of course. Is his temperature normal?'

'Oh yes.' Glibly, in her most professional tone, Nicola added the pulse and respiration rate.

'That seems very satisfactory. I think we'll let him get up today and perhaps—provided the improvement is maintained—he'll be able to leave in another two days.'

Nicola looked at him doubtfully, still puzzled as to why he appeared to be making so much of what was, after all, a not very serious illness. 'Do you think he'll be fit enough to ride his bike?' she asked. 'Oh—I forgot. It's got something the matter with it.'

'The bike's okay. I had a look at it yesterday and there was nothing wrong that a few minutes' work wouldn't put right, even for somebody without the full use of his left hand.' He glanced at his watch. 'Time for surgery. I'll be up to see Steve before I start my calls.'

Nicola had a clinic later that morning but she knew she would be expected to escort Chris when he went upstairs. Fortunately he was also in a hurry and the visit was brief.

'You can get up this afternoon,' he told Steve, 'and tomorrow you can spend pottering around, getting a bit of fresh air perhaps. Provided the weather's warm, you can ride back to West Codden the following day.'

'That's good news, isn't it?' Nicola said cheerfully when he had gone.

'I suppose you can't wait to get rid of me,' Steve said bitterly. He produced a heavy sigh. 'I wouldn't mind so much if you'd been a bit kinder. Don't get me wrong,' he added hastily. 'You've looked after me wonderfully, but you've done it like it was a duty and not because you wanted to.'

'I don't know what else you could expect!' Nicola bit her lip and restrained herself. 'Listen, Steve—' She sat down on the edge of the bed and looked at him earnestly. 'There's no way you and I can put the clock back. The past is over and done with and the future is a different thing altogether. You *must* believe that.'

'I suppose so,' he muttered sulkily. 'It seems a pity, but you certainly sound as though you mean what you say.'

'I mean every word of it, and I'm glad you've had the sense to accept it at last.' Nicola stood up. 'I'll go and get your elevenses.'

As she busied herself in the kitchen she felt more relaxed—if not exactly happier—than she had done for days. And that evening something happened which made her feel even more comfortable in her mind about Steve. There was a telephone call for him.

'Can I speak to him?' said a girl's voice. 'Or is he still in bed?'

'Oh no—he's much better. Who shall I say wants him?'

'I'm Maggie Nixon—Kevin's sister. We all share a flat, you know. I was wondering whether Steve would be able to come back on his motor cycle or whether somebody had better fetch him in the van. I could manage it on Saturday—'

'That won't be necessary. The doctor says he can ride his bike—'

'But there's something wrong with it, isn't there?' the girl asked.

'It's been mended,' Nicola told her hastily. 'Hang on and I'll fetch Steve.'

'Who was that?' Alison enquired curiously when Nicola returned to the sitting-room.

She listened with interest to the brief explanation of the call, and at the end of it merely raised her eyebrows and changed the subject.

'By the way, I think I ought to tell you that your uncle knows about Steve's visit, just in case he should refer to it. I bumped into him when I went out this morning and he asked me if I knew why there was an old motor bike tucked away on the other side of the house. I can't think why he imagined I would know a thing like that but, of course, I *did* know and I put him completely in the picture.'

'What did he say?'

'I leave that to your imagination.'

Nicola laughed and did not press for details. With all her heart she hoped that Dr Hardwick wouldn't mention the matter to her.

He said nothing the following day, and on the afternoon after that Steve would leave. Nicola hoped that the danger would then be past. She examined the weather early that morning and found it warm and sunny, entirely suitable for the cycle ride.

She was not very much looking forward to saying goodbye, fearing reproaches or perhaps even a last-minute attempt to make her change her mind about their future. But when she went upstairs at lunch-time the flat was strangely quiet. The spare room was empty and so were the other rooms. Steve had gone.

Nicola went into her own room and closed the door. Her face looked back at her seriously from the mirror, the eyes wide and very much afraid of what fate might have in store for her in the way of heart-break. She now knew that she had never loved Steve and never could love him. Chris had come into her life and Steve's chances of a reconciliation had melted like frost in the sun.

But Chris would go out of it again, and quite soon too. He would vanish to the closed world of the hospital, there to pursue the surgical career on which his hopes were set. He would be unlikely to spare another thought for the nurse attached to the practice where he had temporarily worked.

She was very silent at supper that evening, and Alison—who was inclined to be in a jubilant mood—gave her several uneasy glances. They had just finished the washing-up when the bell rang downstairs at the private door.

To Nicola's astonishment it was Dr Hardwick.

'Has that young good-for-nothing gone?' he demanded, looking about him suspiciously as they reached the top of the stairs.

'Yes, Uncle.' She hastened to usher him into the sitting-room. 'Come and sit down. We've got some of that sherry you like.'

'You look tired, James,' Alison told him. 'I would have thought things would be easier now that you have another doctor in the practice.'

'So they are, in a way.' He accepted a glass of sherry. 'But there's one snag—he can't take night calls. Or, to put it slightly differently, he can't take them while he's living at the local.' He took a sip of his drink and looked at his sister with a curious expression on his face.

If it had been anyone but her Uncle James, Nicola would have thought that he was a little embarrassed.

'And even if he found somewhere else to live,' he went on, 'there'd be the problem of not being able to use a car just now.'

'Seems an insoluble difficulty.'

'That's what I thought—until this week.' He paused to enjoy his drink. 'This is really very good sherry.'

'It's left from what you gave us last Christmas.' Alison flung him a challenging look. 'Come on, James,' she admonished him. 'You've got something on your mind and I'd very much like to know what it is. You didn't drop in here this evening just to pay a casual call.'

'Er—no. I have, as a matter of fact, got something I want to discuss with you. You have, I think, got two spare rooms, one of which is a bedroom and the other a sitting-room?'

Nicola stared at her uncle and then glanced at Alison as she confirmed it. There had been an odd note in her voice and it wasn't hard to guess that the same thought was in both their minds.

'I think you've caught my meaning?' Dr Hardwick said blandly.

Alison got up to replenish his glass. 'Perhaps I have, but I think you should put it into words.'

'Very well.' He put the tips of his long, elegant fingers together and looked at her over them. 'Our young assistant needs somewhere to live which would be more convenient than where he is now. You need some safeguard against another overnight visit from Steve Paynton and, if I might suggest it, an additional source of income might not come amiss.'

'And that all adds up to—?'

'Letting your two spare rooms to Chris Felgate, of course. Nicola can drive him if he gets called out in the night, and he'll be a lot more comfortable than he is at the pub. So how about it?'

'Good heavens, James!' Alison burst out. 'I can't possibly answer that without turning it over in my mind first. There's a lot to be considered. For one thing, I've never even thought of having a lodger, though certainly the money would be very welcome.'

'It would only be for a short time.'

'Yes, I suppose so.' Alison looked across at Nicola. 'What's your opinion? You're very closely concerned in this.'

Closely concerned! Nicola's heart was thudding and her face felt hot, but at least she could control her voice.

'I hardly know. It's been sprung on us so suddenly—'

'How else could I approach it except suddenly?' Dr Hardwick demanded. 'It's not the sort of thing anyone could take twenty minutes to lead up to, and in any case I see no necessity for hesitation. It's a very simple matter, surely?'

'Have you said anything to Chris about it?'

'Certainly not. That would have been a very wrong angle of approach.'

'But you think he would like to come here?'

James Hardwick shrugged. 'How should I know? If he's got any sense I should think he'd jump at the chance.'

'It's *your* opinion we're wanting, Nicola,' Alison urged. 'If you don't want me to take a lodger, now's your chance to say so.'

'I—I don't mind.' She forced herself to smile. 'But I hope we don't get too many night calls.'

'So do I.' Alison paused, lost in thought while the others waited. 'All right,' she said eventually. 'I'm willing to give it a trial if Chris is agreeable, but I won't cook for him, James. You must make that quite plain. Doctors eat at all sorts of odd hours and I can't be messed around like that when I'm not used to it.'

'As you wish.' He finished the sherry and rose to his feet. 'I'll tell Chris to come and see you and you must discuss the details in a businesslike way and get everything in order.' With a smile, he gave his sister's shoulder an encouraging pat. 'I'm glad you've decided to be sensible.'

'Sensible!' Alison exclaimed when she had seen him to the door. 'I'm not at all sure about that, but I expect I shall find out in due course. James was always good at getting his own way even when we were children, and Shirley, of course, never stands up to him so he's continued being bossy.'

She went on talking but Nicola wasn't paying

much attention. Her mind was in a turmoil as she imagined what it would be like to have Chris actually living under the same roof, around first thing in the morning and at bedtime, and other times as well very likely.

Would the close proximity improve their relationship? Or would it have the opposite effect?

She went to bed with the question still looming large in her head and lay awake for a long time thinking about it. But in the morning there was the usual rush and she was able to shelve it.

Later on she caught a glimpse of Chris coming downstairs, but he went straight out without appearing to notice her. Alison was out at lunchtime and Nicola had to wait until the evening for information.

'We got everything settled,' Alison said briefly.

'When's he moving in?'

'Tomorrow, after the day's work is finished. Or,' she added grimly, 'he hopes it's finished.'

Alison seemed in a silent mood and Nicola had nothing to say either. They had their meal and washed up, and then some inner restlessness drove Nicola to the telephone to ring up Janet. She had carefully timed her call to fit in with evening visiting and her friend was free to chat for a few minutes.

'I haven't seen you for ages,' Janet said, 'and I'm working late tonight. I shall be off at eight tomorrow, though. How about you coming here and we'll go over to the Bull for a drink?'

The Bull was a small pub nearly opposite the hospital, much used by nurses and doctors, and close enough for 'bleeping' in case of emergency. Nicola had affectionate memories of it and therefore met the suggestion with enthusiasm. Besides, if she started off in good time she would probably be out of the flat when Chris moved in.

'Great!' she said cheerfully. 'Be seeing you then.'

Alison was still in an uncommunicative mood and they went to bed early. The next day Nicola fully expected Chris to make some reference to the change in his circumstances, but the drama occasioned by a patient who fainted in the waiting room, upsetting pot plants, magazines and chairs, delayed the end of surgery. He went off on his round with nothing having been said.

They were busy again in the evening, but as Nicola was tidying up after the last patient he came into the waiting room.

'Were you thinking of fetching my stuff for me from the pub?' he asked.

She looked at him blankly, her hands full of comics. 'I hadn't thought at all, and I'm going out soon. Could you just bring enough for tonight and I'll pick up the rest tomorrow?'

'Okay.' He stood in the doorway, tall and broad-shouldered, a ray of sunshine lighting up his tawny hair, and stared down at Nicola.

'I suppose you're going to meet Steve,' he said coolly, 'just to make sure he's all right.'

'No, I'm not!' Colour flamed in her cheeks. 'And even if I were, it's nothing to do with you.' Her temper bubbling, she hurried on. 'I hope I shan't be expected to give an account of myself every time I go out, now that we're going to be living under the same roof.'

Chris raised his eyebrows. He was maddeningly calm. 'I think that would be a little unreasonable. We shan't see all that much of each other, anyway, since I shall have my own two rooms. Your mother made it clear that I shall be expected to keep to them.'

Nicola shrugged and turned away. How could she ever have been such a fool as to imagine he would be pleased at moving into a new temporary home? No doubt he was thinking nostalgically of the life and noise at the pub which he was going to miss, and the prospect of night calls instead.

She was glad to escape from the flat as soon as possible and she arrived at the hospital just as Janet was taking off her uniform. When she had put on jeans and a thin sweater they crossed the busy road and went into the Bull to join a crowd of nurses and junior doctors who were talking by the bar.

Nicola absorbed the old familiar hospital atmosphere with pleasure, and at the same time felt a little out of it. She did not join in the conversation very much but she was happy just to be there, once again part of a hospital group.

They stayed for some time and then Janet

suggested going back to her flatlet for coffee.

'We haven't had a chance to talk properly,' she said as they waited at the pedestrian crossing. 'How's things?'

When she came out that evening Nicola hadn't wanted to talk about Steve, but she felt differently now and she at once plunged into an account of his visit.

'He actually had bronchitis at your flat? What a nerve!' Janet's darkened eyebrows rose dramatically.

'He wasn't well enough to ride back the first night and it was late; besides, the bike was giving trouble. And then in the morning he was worse. He stayed for several days.'

'I suppose you had to look after him. How did you feel about that?'

'I hated it,' Nicola said tersely.

They had crossed the road and were approaching the huge block of hospital apartments. As they dodged through a party of nurses coming off late duty, Janet continued to discuss Steve's visit.

'Didn't it seem strange to see him at the flat again? It must have brought everything back to you rather uncomfortably.'

'Well—yes, but not quite in the way you mean. I've stopped being angry with Steve for what he did to me and now I mostly just feel sorry for him. And not always that,' Nicola added hastily. 'He says the shop at West Codden is doing quite well and I really believe he's settled down.'

Janet unlocked her front door and ushered Nicola into the large bed-sitting room. Continuing the discussion she went into her tiny kitchen and plugged in the kettle.

'I can't help thinking Steve would have done better for himself if he hadn't chickened out of getting married. He obviously needs a girl like you to take him in hand.'

Nicola smiled and sat down in one of the two easy chairs. She thought of Maggie Nixon but decided not to mention her. After all, she didn't actually *know* anything except that Steve liked her cooking.

'It seems funny he should have turned up like that,' Janet went on. 'Didn't he give you even a hint that he'd like to start again?'

Her friend's blue eyes were staring straight at her and there was no possibility of prevarication for Nicola. But it was with the greatest of reluctance that she answered the question.

'Well—yes, he gave me rather more than a hint, actually. But I didn't encourage him, of course.'

'I think you're still fond of him though,' Janet persisted, 'in spite of what you just said, so perhaps there might be some future for you after all. Somebody who needs looking after would really suit you much better than a bossy type like—'

Nicola looked at her in astonishment. 'Like who?' she asked in bewilderment.

'Like Chris Felgate,' Janet said carelessly.

CHAPTER TEN

'CHRIS FELGATE?' Nicola repeated stupidly.

'Don't pretend you've never heard of him,' Janet said with a smile.

'I'm not pretending anything of the sort.' Nicola accepted a mug of coffee. 'I was just surprised that you should mention him, that's all. I know you nursed him when he had his accident but I didn't think—'

'That I'd met him since? Well, actually it was only the other day, but we remembered each other at once and he told me all about working with your uncle as a stop-gap until his arm is better. I do think you've been a dark horse, Nicky, not ringing up with an interesting little item of news like that.'

'It didn't occur to me that it *was* interesting,' Nicola told her with as much nonchalance as she could manage. 'And I still think it's extraordinary that you should have run across each other. He hardly ever goes into Debenbridge.'

Janet sat down in the armchair opposite and balanced her coffee on the top of a pile of magazines beside it. 'This was his day off and he was doing a bit of exploring. We bumped into one another outside the coffee shop where you and I sometimes meet. It happened to be my free day too and so we had lunch together.'

Nicola took a cautious sip of the hot dark liquid. Her throat felt dry and shock seemed to have numbed her brain, but it didn't need much intelligence to work out that the day Janet had lunched with Chris was the same one on which he had taken her—Nicola—to the Garden House. And he hadn't said a word about meeting Janet.

'He seems tremendously fit now,' Janet went on. 'I never saw anyone get over an accident so quickly. I asked him whether, now that he was into general practice, he might consider giving up his surgical ambitions. He just about tore me apart! He really is dead keen, isn't he? And he must have made a wonderful impression on Mr Bradshaw or the job wouldn't have been kept for him.'

'It's a bit unusual,' Nicola agreed, 'but Mr Bradshaw makes his own rules.' She hesitated, aware that there was something Janet couldn't possibly know, and that she would have to be told. 'I've got another item of news which I expect you'll find interesting.' She tried to speak lightly, as though it wasn't of much importance to her personally.

Her friend looked at her expectantly and she ploughed on. 'Chris is moving into the flat this evening, to occupy the two rooms which were to have been for Steve and me. It was fixed up by Uncle James so he could take night calls, and also to keep Steve out, I think.'

For a moment Janet seemed too taken aback

to comment and Nicola received the impression that she was having to control her voice and expression as much as she herself had just had to do.

'How do you feel about that?' she asked eventually. 'Won't it bring it all back to you? I mean, having a—a comparative stranger living in the rooms where you'd expected to start your married life?'

Nicola finished her coffee with a gulp. 'You're absolutely determined to make me think sentimentally about Steve, aren't you? Can't I knock it into your head that I don't want to? It's too late for that now.'

'I wouldn't have thought so,' Janet said obstinately.

'Okay then, we'd better talk about something else.'

But although both girls tried to restore the friendly atmosphere which had prevailed earlier, they were not entirely successful and Nicola soon left to go home.

Out of doors, the soft night air enfolded her in a soothing embrace as she walked slowly towards the car park. Lost in thought, she was unaware of the city sights and sounds—the cathedral spire floodlit against the dark sky, the town hall announcing that it was eleven o'clock with sonorous clangs, and, near at hand, the great hospital with its long rows of lighted windows.

The short drive back to Moresham was soon accomplished, though she did not hurry. She let herself in quietly and went up to the flat. The door of the spare bedroom stood wide open with an airline bag in the middle of the floor, still packed. It didn't look as though the lodger had been there very long.

In the sitting-room the television was on and the door shut, but some slight sound from the kitchen aroused Nicola's curiosity and she went to investigate.

Chris was there, pouring beaten eggs into a frying pan with great competence.

'Use of kitchen is included,' he said cheerfully, 'so there's no need to look at me like that.'

Nicola pulled herself together. 'I wasn't looking at you like anything. I was just taken by surprise.'

'Omelettes are my speciality, but I don't expect to have them every night. The trouble was, I got called out as soon as I got here and since you were missing—' his tone was maddeningly reproachful '—I was obliged to walk. Two miles there and two miles back.'

'Exercise is good for you.'

'I'd had enough during the day, thank you. Would you like me to do an omelette for you?'

'No, thanks. I had my meal early and I've been eating crisps since then.'

She watched as he folded the omelette expertly, flipped it on to a hot plate and sat down at the kitchen table. He looked as much at home as though he had lived in the flat all his life.

'Stay and talk to me while I eat,' he invited.

'You can get busy with the coffee if you like. I expect you'd like some too.'

'I've just been drinking coffee—with Janet.' Nicola held her breath as she waited for his answer.

'The blonde nurse who was on my ward? How is she?' Chris asked casually.

'Fine!'

Her back turned, Nicola switched on the percolator and then suddenly swung round to face him. Why didn't he say something about having seen Janet so recently? And why on earth couldn't she herself manage to introduce the subject?

Chris looked up from his omelette and glanced at her. 'You've got a most peculiar expression on your face, Nicola. Is something wrong?'

'No, of course not. Why should there be?'

'I can't imagine. Perhaps you're just tired. After all, you work pretty hard and you haven't had a summer holiday yet, have you?'

'N-no. I didn't want to spend the money when I thought I was getting married. I'll arrange something during the autumn—October perhaps. It's often a lovely month.'

'I haven't experienced an English fall since I was a teenager,' Chris said conversationally.

To her relief he began to talk about the autumn in Canada and nothing more was said about Janet, or Nicola looking tired, or anything in the least controversial. Before long she was able to escape to bed.

After that, Nicola somehow managed to avoid being alone with him, and as the first week slipped by she was obliged to admit that he was surprisingly unobtrusive. He got his own breakfast, had lunch out at a pub, and cooked his evening meal long after Nicola and her mother had finished. There were no night calls.

At the beginning of the second week he put his head in at the office door one evening when Nicola was sorting through some cards.

'Hi, there! I've got news for you.' And as she turned in surprise he continued in a satisfied tone, 'I thought you might be interested to know that Alison has taken pity on me and is providing my dinner in future.'

Alison! Nicola gasped and wondered what had overtaken her normally reserved mother. She had said quite definitely that she wasn't going to cook for the lodger.

'I didn't think you needed her pity,' she said sharply. 'You seemed to me to be coping very well.'

'I'd rather not have to bother, all the same.' And he went away.

That night they had the first emergency call. Nicola was awake instantly and she had her dressing-gown on when Chris knocked on her door. He looked unfamiliar and somehow younger in pale blue pyjamas trimmed with navy, his hair on end and his normally brilliant blue eyes clouded with sleep.

'Who is it?' she asked quickly.

'Afraid I've got a shock for you.' His voice was very grave. 'It's your problem patient, Mrs Riley. She's taken an overdose.'

'Oh *no!*' Nicola snatched up an armful of clothes as he disappeared towards his own room. 'I'll be ready in a sec.'

In less than five minutes they were speeding along the deserted road in the direction of the housing estate. There were lights on all over the neat little house which was their objective, and as Nicola drew up outside, the front door opened instantly.

Martin Riley was a stocky figure in jeans and a bulky sweater. His receding dark hair was wildly untidy and his face pale.

'Thank God you're here,' was his greeting. 'I didn't know whether to ring the doctor or the hospital, and as you're so much nearer—'

'Which room?' Chris was half-way up the stairs. 'Do you know what she took and how many tablets?'

'The front one, Doctor. It'd be her sleeping tablets, I reckon. She didn't have anything else.'

Nicola followed them quickly. She felt cold and sick with fear and clung desperately to the only hopeful element in the whole tragic situation. It was early in the night—no more than two o'clock—and Mrs Riley couldn't have had the tablets in her system for so very long.

She was completely unaware of the fussily pretty bedroom and the monotonous voice of the patient's husband, who didn't seem able to stop talking. Her eyes were on Chris who stood by the bed, his fingers on Mrs Riley's pulse.

He looked up and met Nicola's anxious gaze. 'Strong black coffee. And as soon as you've made it, come and help me here.'

She hurried as much as she could but the kitchen was unfamiliar and at first she couldn't find the coffee. As she hunted for it she could hear Mr Riley on the telephone, asking for an ambulance.

Back upstairs, she found Chris had dragged Mrs Riley upright in bed and was holding her there. As Nicola joined him on the other side he began shouting into the patient's ear.

'Wake up, Mrs Riley—wake up—*wake up*!'

But she was deeply unconscious, a completely dead weight against their arms, and Mr Riley, hovering in the background, was almost wringing his hands in his distress.

'Where's her dressing-gown?' Chris asked him.

'Here—' He snatched up a pink frilly garment and held it out.

As they struggled to get her limp arms into the sleeves, Nicola's eyes alighted on a half-empty bottle on the bedside table. Perhaps it had been full a short time ago; their total lack of success suggested a large dose.

The coffee was rapidly cooling and Mrs Riley moaned faintly, but her eyes remained closed and it didn't look as though the stimulant would be any use. Nicola's arms ached unbearably but

Chris seemed tireless as they fought to drag their patient back to the life she hadn't considered worth living. It seemed an age before the ambulance drew up in front of the house, although Nicola realised afterwards that the men had been very quick.

'I'm going with her,' Martin Riley said.

Nicola looked at him sharply. 'What about Gary?'

'Oh God—I'd forgotten him. It's lucky he's slept through all this. Can't you take him, Nurse, and look after him for a bit?'

'It's *your* job to take care of your little son, Mr Riley,' Chris told him firmly. 'And there's no point in going with your wife. You wouldn't be able to stay with her while they were getting rid of the drug.' Deliberately he added, 'I don't think you would want to either.'

'You'll be able to keep in close touch by telephone,' Nicola put in, 'and you can take Gary to his grandma in the morning and then go on to the hospital.'

They left the man still looking dazed and drove away. As they reached the corner Nicola said suddenly, 'What's the prognosis? Has she got a hope?'

'Plenty, I'd say. She'll probably be perfectly okay when they've washed her out.'

'Perfectly?' Nicola's voice was bitter. 'That's an odd word to use. She'll still be desperately unhappy and—and it's all my fault.'

'Your fault?' Chris turned to look at her.

'Don't be such a fool—of course you're not to blame. If anyone is, it's her husband for putting so much pressure on her to get rid of the new baby. Let's hope tonight will teach him a lesson.'

Nicola beat her hands on the steering wheel, causing the little car to swerve dangerously. 'But I *am* to blame! I told you I handled her badly and I never followed up that visit in any way or checked to see whether she'd seen a doctor.'

'Watch it!' Chris warned. 'I'd like to get back in one piece if you don't mind.'

But Nicola was past caring. Reaction had set in and the tears were streaming down her face so that she could scarcely see. It was a long time since she had come into close contact with a would-be suicide—not since her hospital days— and the experience had upset her badly.

'For God's sake!' Chris exclaimed. 'Stop for a few minutes and let's get you sorted out.'

She drew up obediently. They were near the turning to the church where a large elm overhung the road and would have hidden them from onlookers had there been any to see. As Nicola leaned back with a sigh, Chris stretched across her and switched off the engine.

Immediately such a profound silence settled over them that the sound of their breathing seemed abnormally loud. An owl swept over the car on noiseless wings but neither of them noticed it, nor did they see the cat which appeared suddenly on the churchyard wall and looked at them curiously.

'You little fool,' Chris said roughly. 'You're supposed to be a nurse. You shouldn't be so vulnerable.'

'I—I can't help it.'

'It's that ridiculously tender heart of yours.' He slid his arm along the back of the seat and turned her face towards him with his other hand. Very gently he kissed her wet eyes, first one and then the other. With a sob Nicola buried her face in his shoulder.

It was wonderfully comforting to feel his arms about her, and when he stopped being gentle and became demanding she responded eagerly, her grief forgotten and her whole body exulting at the close contact with his.

'Better now?' Chris asked softly after a while.

'Oh yes, thank you. I'm sorry I was such an idiot.'

He released her slowly after a last lingering kiss. Then, to her surprise he got out and walked round to her side of the car. 'Move over,' he ordered.

'But—' She looked up at him in bewilderment.

'You're in no state to drive and I've been yearning to have a go for a long time. I know I can manage perfectly well, if only your uncle and the police would realise that.'

With the fingers of his left hand free, he could easily operate the gear lever, and did so with great competence. Confidently he drove down the village street and into the drive of the doctor's house.

'I shall probably get the all-clear for driving again very soon anyway,' he said casually.

'You what?' Nicola asked in surprise. 'But surely your plaster isn't due to be taken off yet?'

'No, not exactly, but I'm getting a new one— much lighter. I've already been to the garage and picked out an automatic, and provided I stick to that I don't think anyone will raise objections.'

She was silent as she digested the information and found it unpalatable. He wouldn't be dependent on her any more, which would undoubtedly please him immensely, but what did she feel about it?

Refusing to answer the question, she led the way indoors, accepted his cool good-night kiss and went to bed. But she did not sleep for a long time.

The following morning her first thought was for Mrs Riley. A telephone call to the hospital told her that the patient was now considered out of danger and she lost no time in telling Chris.

'That's great!' He paused with his hand on the knob of the bathroom door. 'It's a sobering thought,' he continued, his tone much more serious, 'that if Mr Riley hadn't needed to go to the toilet his wife would almost certainly be dead now. I hope they both realise what a near thing it was.'

'I'm sure they do, but—' Nicola hesitated. 'It hasn't really solved anything. She's still got to face up to an unwanted pregnancy and, if it's like last time, a lot of misery and discomfort.'

'She'll get psychiatric help at the hospital and perhaps something can be done to make her nine months less unhappy. There was a wonderful drug we used in Canada. Who's her doctor?'

'Peter Featherstone.'

'I'll have a word with him.'

Nicola said no more. The case was out of her hands now and she could view it more objectively. Fortunately very few unwilling mothers-to-be attempted suicide, and she couldn't really be blamed for not guessing it might happen.

Life continued as before, except that she saw more of Chris now that he ate his evening meal with them, a circumstance which quite clearly meant a great deal more to her than it did to him. Alison seemed to enjoy catering for him, in spite of all she had said against it before he moved in. She praised his good appetite and told him it made cooking worth while. Observing them and their happy relationship, Nicola could only marvel and wonder why she couldn't be equally relaxed with him.

There was universal rejoicing when he appeared with his new lightweight plaster, following it the next day with a smart red car fitted with an automatic gearbox.

'Now he'll really be able to pull his weight,' Dr Featherstone commented in a satisfied tone.

'Unfortunately,' said Dr Hardwick, 'that means he'll soon be gone.'

'You really think so, James?' The junior partner looked doubtful. 'Personally, I'm inclined to think we may be able to keep him. He's settled in so very well.'

'We shall have to wait and see.'

Nicola, overhearing their conversation, felt even more pessimistic than her uncle about the prospect of Chris staying on, but she kept her thoughts to herself. The two doctors left together, still discussing the matter, and she continued with her end-of-the-day chores.

As she tidied Dr Hardwick's surgery, Chris looked in.

'I shall be late for the meal tonight. Got an emergency call. Tell your mother I'm sorry to mess her around.'

He went off, obviously delighted with his new-found independence, and Nicola went upstairs. To her surprise there was no table laid and her mother was hunting in the fridge in an agitated manner.

'I'm all on the drag tonight, Nicola.' She located some chops and extracted them. 'I've had a worrying phone call from Hillsley.'

Hillsley was the sheep farm high up in the Yorkshire Dales where Nicola's grandparents lived. Although past retiring age, the elderly man still worked hard and managed to make a living from his rough acres.

'Your grandfather's had a slight stroke,' Alison continued, 'and Mother naturally wants me to go up. James, too, of course, if he can get away, but I expect that will take a little time to fix up.'

'There's nothing to stop you going off tomorrow,' Nicola said when she had exclaimed in distress at the news. 'I expect the library will release you?'

'Oh yes—no problem there. It's *you* I'm bothered about, dear. I can't possibly leave you and Chris alone in the flat. It wouldn't do at all—'

'Oh, Mum—don't be so absurd! We'd be okay.'

'I hope you would, but I shouldn't be at all easy in my mind about it. In a village you can't be too careful. However,' she flung the chops into a frying pan and turned up the heat, 'I've got it all taken care of. Janet's coming to stay for a few days. She was quite pleased, actually. Isn't that lucky?'

CHAPTER ELEVEN

'JANET coming to stay?' Chris sounded, in Nicola's ears, both surprised and pleased.

She had given him the news of her grandfather's stroke while they waited for the evening meal and he had gone at once to her mother to express his sympathy and do all he could to allay her fears. It was while they were waiting for the overdue evening meal that she added the information about Janet.

'It was my mother's idea,' Nicola said, adding in an unguarded moment, 'I suppose you realise why she wants me to have a friend to stay?'

Chris stared at her. 'I haven't a clue, unless it was because she thought you'd be lonely.'

'Nothing like that.' She forced a smile. 'She imagines it wouldn't be proper to leave us on our own.'

His astonishment was ludicrous. 'Proper! I didn't think anyone bothered about that sort of thing these days.'

'Mum's a bit old-fashioned. I told her she'd got nothing to worry about, of course.'

He was still looking at her but now his expression changed. There was laughter in his eyes as he said softly, 'I shouldn't be too sure about that if I were you.' He held her gaze until, to her annoyance, she was obliged to look away.

'But with two girls around,' Chris went on smoothly, 'I shall be so overwhelmed by feminine attractions that both of you will be perfectly safe.'

He was mocking her—that was very plain. Furious with him, and herself too, Nicola stormed out of the room.

She was up early in the morning, to drive her mother to Debenbridge station. Janet, who had a free half-day, arrived in time for the evening meal, having travelled from the city by bus.

Chris was at home and it was he who answered the bell. Nicola heard them coming up the stairs, talking cheerfully together. After the girls had greeted each other he followed Janet to Alison's room—which she was to occupy—and stayed there for a while, continuing the conversation. Busy in the kitchen, Nicola could hear their voices but not what was being said, and she was obliged to wrestle with a quite absurd sensation of being left out of it.

'This is going to be fun,' Janet said, her blue eyes sparkling, as the three of them sat down round the table.

'Except having to get up practically at dawn when you're on early duty,' Nicola pointed out. 'What time will you have to leave here?'

'About six-fifty.' Janet shuddered. 'I mustn't miss the seven o'clock bus.'

'If you do find you're in danger of that,' Chris accepted a helping of steak and kidney pie, made by Alison the evening before, and piled his plate with vegetables, 'I'll run you into Debenbridge myself.'

'It's absolutely *super* that you can drive again. Is that red car outside yours? It's much too sporty-looking to belong to either of the other doctors.'

Chris acknowledged his ownership with a boyish eagerness which Nicola found intensely touching. How he must have hated the occasions when he had been driven around by herself in the Mini. She was not surprised when he offered to take Janet for a short spin at the end of the meal, and at once turned down her friend's half-hearted offer of help with the washing-up.

'Not tonight. Tomorrow we'll get ourselves organised, but I don't want you to start domestic chores as soon as you get here.'

To her surprise, Chris intervened. 'Leave the washing-up, Nicola,' he ordered, 'and we'll all get down to it when we come back.'

Nicola would have liked to occupy herself with the job while they were out, but she found herself meekly falling in with his instructions. And then, as she wandered restlessly about the flat, the telephone rang with a message for him and he was obliged to go out again as soon as he returned.

'I discovered something when we were out,' Janet said, drying a handful of cutlery. 'Next Sunday is Chris's day off and it happens to be my free weekend. Don't you think it would be a good idea for us all to go out for the day? If the weather's warm we might take bathing things.'

She did not seem to notice Nicola's lack of enthusiasm and immediately put the suggestion to Chris when he eventually came back to the flat after making some late calls.

'It's okay with me, but you girls will have to choose the place. I don't know much about the coast near here.'

'Sandbeach would be best,' Janet decided. 'It's got a lovely beach just like the name suggests. Oh—!' She broke off abruptly. 'I forgot—that's where you met Nicola, isn't it?'

Nicola had been laying the table for breakfast in order to save time in the morning, but her busy hands were stilled as she felt her whole body becoming rigid. Nerving herself, she turned slowly round and looked at Chris.

But he did not meet her gaze. He was leaning back against the fridge, his eyes on the toes of his well-polished shoes.

'I believe so,' he said calmly, 'but it was just before I got knocked on the head and my memories of the place are a bit—muddled.'

Nicola found she had been holding her breath. Still not entirely sure how much he had remembered about that weekend, she nevertheless felt herself slowly relaxing. He had either forgotten what had happened in her room at the Belmont or he regarded it as totally unimportant, the sort of incident that was likely to occur between a man and a girl in such circumstances.

She had better do the same.

Perhaps because she wasn't looking forward to Sunday's outing, the week began to flash past at considerable speed. Her mother phoned to say that her grandfather was better but she didn't want to hurry back if all was well at home.

'Fine!' Nicola told her. 'Janet's fitted in well and everything's going on just the same as if you were here, except that I do the cooking and I don't mind that.'

'I hope the others are helping you as much as they can?'

'Oh yes. You haven't a thing to worry about, Mum—honestly.'

'In that case, I'll definitely stay over the weekend. Goodbye, dear—take care.'

Take care . . . Nicola's thoughts were bitter as she replaced the receiver. It was too late to be careful not to fall in love with Chris and nothing else seemed to matter very much.

By Saturday morning her enthusiasm for the visit to Sandbeach had reached zero point. She even suggested to Janet that three was an awkward number and that she—Nicola—might drop out, but her friend had indignantly refused to consider it.

'Don't be silly, Nicky. It would spoil the whole day if we had to worry about you being left at home on your own. Of course you must come.'

And so, while Janet slept late, Nicola took her shopping basket and went out to the village supermarket to purchase what was required for the picnic. Loaded with fruit and rolls, pâté and cheeses, she returned to the flat to find Chris in the kitchen making coffee and Janet, wearing a black embroidered caftan, sitting at the table.

Perhaps Nicola was super-sensitive at the moment but it seemed to her that what had been an animated conversation before she appeared somehow fell apart when she went in with her basket. She had almost thought she caught the name 'Steve' and she wondered what Janet had been saying. Was she still clinging to her sentimental hope that Nicola and Steve would be reunited?

With an effort she thrust aside her depression and cheerfully displayed her shopping for their approval.

'All we need now,' said Janet, 'is a fine day.'

When Nicola woke in the morning her first thought was the weather. There was no sunshine creeping round her curtains but when she looked out she found an early mist which would soon give way to clear skies and sun. In the meantime it was chilly and she put on—by pure chance— the same linen trousers and yellow top which she had worn at Sandbeach on her previous visit with Chris.

At first he didn't seem to notice. It was not until they were both on the landing, about to follow Janet downstairs, that he suddenly looked Nicola up and down with a strange expression on his face.

'I've seen you dressed like that before,' he said slowly.

Her heart missed a beat but she managed to answer carelessly, 'So? I often wear these clothes.'

'You haven't had them on since I moved into the flat, and before that you were mostly in uniform.'

'I really can't remember whether I've worn them or not. It doesn't matter, does it?'

Chris had recovered his poise. He said with a carelessness which matched Nicola's, 'It seemed to just for a moment, but I can't imagine why.'

She turned towards the stairs in response to Janet's call from below. 'Aren't you two ever coming down?' As she began to descend she felt furious with herself because she hadn't selected her outfit more carefully. It was bad enough to be going to Sandbeach with Chris, without choosing clothes which were likely to trigger off memories which she would prefer to remain in the limbo of his subconscious.

Janet was looking very attractive in a blue and white summer dress with a light anorak over it, and Chris wore shorts with a lime green shirt which showed up his tan and the brightness of his tawny hair. As they got into the red car they made a colourful picture which earned interested glances from the few passers-by.

'One of us had better sit in front on the way there, and the other coming back,' Janet suggested. 'Shall we toss up?'

'There's no need for that,' Nicola said quickly. 'You have first turn.'

She was very quiet as she sat alone in the back, though Janet turned round several times and tried to draw her into the conversation. When they reached the outskirts of Sandbeach memories swept over her and the recollection of that day in June was as clear as though it had been only last week.

If only she could be sure that it would remain for ever lost in the dark recesses of Chris's mind!

By the time they had parked the car the sun had at last managed to burst through the mist and a sparkling sea lay before them. It was such a lovely day that even Nicola's black mood responded to it and she made up her mind to enjoy the sunshine and bathing.

Fortunately she had brought a bikini instead of the one-piece outfit she had purchased at Sandbeach, and Chris made no comment. They bathed at once, and then ate their lunch and went in the water again after a suitable interval.

Afterwards they lay on the beach, Janet in the middle, and lazed in the sun. Suddenly Chris raised himself on his elbow and looked down at the slender blonde girl next to him.

'I reckon you've done enough sun-bathing for today, Janet. You don't look to me as though you're used to it.'

'I'm okay,' she protested, turning a flushed face towards him. 'I can't feel the slightest sign of burning.'

Magnificent in his own established tan, he was gazing at her with almost a tender look in his eyes. 'Be sensible, love,' he said softly. 'You won't feel it until tonight and then it'll be hell.' And he reached out and covered her legs with his own towel.

'What about Nicky?'

Chris glanced across to Janet's other side. 'Dark girls don't have to worry so much. It's the blondes who have to be really careful.'

No one made any further comment but for Nicola the harmonious atmosphere which had so far prevailed was spoilt. She was glad when Janet announced that she was thirsty and suggested finding somewhere for a drink.

Chris glanced at his watch. 'They'll just about be open, I should think. Let's get dressed then.'

They had only been walking along the promenade for a short distance when Nicola realised they would soon pass the Belmont Hotel. To her horror Janet drew attention to it.

'Do you think that place has an ordinary bar tucked away somewhere?'

'Yes, I believe so.'

He had answered with extreme naturalness and did not seem to be aware that he had said anything out of the ordinary. To Nicola's relief he turned down the old-fashioned place with its ultra-respectable front and suggested going somewhere else.

They had to walk nearly to the end of the promenade before they found what they wanted.

The Fisherman's Arms was old-fashioned too, but in an entirely different sort of way, with dark crowded bars, horse brasses hanging from the ceiling and darts being played. They were all thirsty now, and lazy after their swimming, and for a while they were content just to enjoy the long cool drinks.

'Let's eat here,' Chris said. 'The bar food looks good.'

It was late when they left and they were a long way from the car park, but there was no need to hurry and the air was cool and fresh after the heat of the inn. Although the short season was nearing its end, the promenade was still strung with fairy lights which shimmered on the surface of the dark sea.

'This is lovely.' Janet lifted her face to the gentle breeze. 'A perfect ending to the day.'

Perhaps she wasn't looking where she was going, or maybe it was too dark to see the large stone left in her path by some careless child. Whatever the reason, she stumbled suddenly, clutched at Chris's arm but failed to regain her balance. The next moment she was sitting on the promenade with one foot twisted under her and laughing at her own clumsiness.

'I've had nothing stronger than shandy so it can't be that!'

'Have you hurt yourself?' Chris asked.

'No, of course not.' She stood up quickly and then winced. 'Oh dear—perhaps I have—'

Nicola looked round and spotted a nearby

seat. 'Come and sit down for a minute. I expect you've twisted your ankle.' She held out a supporting arm.

Chris kicked the offending stone over the edge of the promenade and then joined them. 'Which one is it?' He touched Janet's left ankle lightly. 'This one, I think.'

'Yes. It feels as though it's swelling already,' she told him ruefully. 'I wish I could take my sandal off but I suppose I'd better not.'

'It would be wiser to keep it on at present.' He put his hand in his pocket and pulled out a large clean handkerchief, which he handed to Nicola. 'Go and dip this in the sea for me, please, and bring it back thoroughly wet.'

When she returned he was still feeling the injured ankle and looking rather serious. 'You don't think it's broken, do you?' Nicola asked in alarm as he began his bandaging.

'I hope not, but there is the possibility of a hair-line fracture.' He looked up into Janet's face. 'I'm afraid you ought to have it X-rayed, just to make sure.'

'Tonight?' she exclaimed. 'Oh no, I don't want to bother. It may be quite all right in the morning.'

'That's not very likely, even if it's only a sprain. You won't be much use in the ward if you have to hobble about, so you'll almost certainly have to take a day or two off, and you might just as well have it properly examined.'

Seeing rebellion in her expression, he added

quietly, 'It's no good looking like that, Janet, because I'm going to insist.'

She raised her eyebrows and then smiled. 'I can see you're used to getting your own way so I'd better give in gracefully. You're quite capable of driving me straight to the hospital whether I want to go or not.'

'I'm glad you've summed up the situation so accurately.' Chris turned to Nicola. 'I'll go and fetch the car and you can wait here with Janet.'

As soon as he had left them, striding off at a tremendous speed, both girls burst out simultaneously. Janet's, 'What an infuriating thing to happen!' overlapped Nicola's, 'It *is* a shame—I'm so sorry.'

'I still think it will be better after a night's rest,' Janet went on mutinously, 'but it's obviously no good arguing with Chris. Is he always as bossy?'

'Oh yes. The patients like it, of course, because it gives them confidence.'

'I'm not sure that I do, even though I suppose you could call me a patient at the moment.' She paused and then added with a rush of intimacy, 'I'd been beginning to think I could fancy him quite a lot, but I'm not one of those girls who like being dictated to. Are you?'

'No!' Nicola told her with quite unnecessary emphasis.

'I expect that's why you got on so well with Steve. No one could call *him* dynamic.'

They relapsed into silence and before long Chris appeared with the car. Helped by both of them Janet was soon settled—once more in the front seat—and they set off for Debenbridge. No one spoke very much on the journey and Nicola's thoughts were undisturbed. They were mostly concerned with the immediate future, which seemed to her a great deal more worrying than either of the others appeared to have realised.

Her mother would probably be back on Tuesday. It seemed likely that Janet would have several days off work even if she had only sprained her ankle. She would have to rest and be waited on, and she would certainly expect to stay on at the flat, since she would be unaware of Mrs Craven's imminent return. Nicola hadn't mentioned it because she didn't know anything definite.

But when they reached the Accident Unit, the problem was solved for her.

The unit was busy with a crop of Sunday evening accidents and they had to wait some time. Even after Janet was ushered into a cubicle she was not seen by a doctor for at least ten minutes. Then she had to join the queue for X-rays and there was another long wait. But at last the Casualty Sister approached them with a purposeful air.

'I think you are with Nurse Martin, aren't you?' And when they confirmed it, she went on, 'There's no need for you to wait any longer. We've decided to keep her in overnight, since she's one of our own girls and the ankle is very painful. She may even have to stay in the sick bay for a few days.'

'Is there a fracture?' Chris asked.

'No, fortunately, but it's a very bad sprain and needs care. There's no question of her returning to duty until it's really better.'

'She's been staying with me—out at Moresham—and all her things are there—' Nicola began.

'We can provide all she requires for the night. Perhaps you can make some arrangement for bringing her own possessions in for her.'

Janet was sitting in a wheelchair and trying to look resigned. 'Isn't it sickening!' she exclaimed. 'I'm afraid you'll have to do my packing for me, Nicky, and then take the clothes to my flatlet, if you wouldn't mind. Perhaps they'll let me out tomorrow,' she added hopefully.

'Of course I will—tomorrow afternoon probably. And if I don't find you there I'll come to the hospital with your toilet things.' And with warm sympathy Nicola ended, 'Poor Janet—it's a horrible ending to the day.'

'You'll be on your own now, you two.' Janet looked from one to the other with smiling eyes. 'Be good!'

'But of course,' Chris said smoothly.

CHAPTER TWELVE

THERE WAS now no need for Nicola to sit in the back of the car. As she got in the front beside Chris she was aware of tension—her own, not his. He appeared to be entirely at his ease and chatted cheerfully all the way back to Moresham.

'I really enjoyed that visit to the Accident Unit,' he said, 'except for being sorry for poor Janet, of course. I was Casualty Officer at my last post in Canada and this evening really brought it home to me how much I'd been missing the hospital atmosphere.'

'I missed it too,' Nicola told him, 'when I first started to work in the practice. But I like being in contact with whole families of patients,' she added defiantly. 'You really get to know them.'

'I can appreciate that,' Chris said thoughtfully, 'but it doesn't make up for not having the excitement and intense interest of surgery.'

It was late when they reached the village and there was no one to witness their return to the doctor's house without Janet. Her mother would have been glad of that, Nicola reflected. Upstairs, nothing could have been less worthy of gossip. Chris said a quick good night and vanished into his room, and Nicola started to unpack the picnic things, knowing that she would

164

hate to have to do it in the morning.

She was busy with her unattractive job, tipping rubbish into the pedal bin and rinsing out the flasks and mugs, when a voice spoke suddenly from the doorway. Chris stood there in a bright blue terry towelling robe, his bare legs very brown and his face unsmiling.

'You're surely not doing housework tonight?'

'Not housework,' Nicola explained as calmly as she could when her breathing was so uneven. 'I'm only tidying a few odds and ends away. Did you want something?'

'Only to see what you were up to. I could hear you clattering from my room.'

'Well, now you've seen, you can go to bed and leave me to finish in peace.'

She hadn't meant to speak so sharply. It was because she was tired out after the long and difficult day. And also because Chris stood there, so near and yet a million miles away, and she was conscious in every fibre of her being of the assault of his male aura on her senses.

'For God's sake—!' he said explosively. 'What's the matter with you, Nicola? You've been in a foul mood all day. If Janet hadn't been so happy and so obviously enjoying herself, it would have spoilt the outing for us all.'

'That's a horrible thing to say!' she flung at him, shutting the fridge door with a bang. 'If you really want to know, I wasn't at all keen on going to Sandbeach but Janet wouldn't agree to my dropping out. I think three is a thoroughly awkward number for an outing—'

'It's that all right,' he said grimly. 'Why didn't you ask Steve to come along as well?'

Nicola stared at him, her eyes dilating. 'Steve?'

'From something Janet said I got the impression you and he might be coming together again.'

'Janet had no right to hint anything of the sort.' Nicola was scarlet with anger.

'But it's natural she should take an interest, since she's your best friend. As for me—well, I was rather closely involved in your affairs at one time. In fact, I became for a short time a sort of substitute Steve. Remember?'

They looked at each other, the man with his jaw thrust out, the girl aghast and bordering on panic.

'*I* remember,' she said when she could control herself sufficiently to speak, 'but I thought—that is, I wasn't sure how much you'd forgotten about—Sandbeach.'

'It's been coming back to me slowly, like catching glimpses of things through swirling mist, but it wasn't until today that I remembered the lot. I think it was seeing you wearing that gear which triggered it off, and then, of course, I immediately recognised the hotel where we stayed.'

'You were very kind to me,' Nicola said in a low voice. 'I shall always be grateful to you.'

'That's extremely good of you.' The mocking tone she knew well was back in his voice. 'No doubt your intentions are excellent but, personally, I don't believe a word of it.'

'You don't believe it?'

'No. It's hardly the sort of weekend a girl like you would want to go on being grateful about. I'm quite sure you wish I'd never remembered it.'

'If you really want to know,' her anger was bubbling again and she hurled the words at him as though they had been a missile, 'I would have been extremely glad if your amnesia on that particular point had lasted for ever. I should be obliged if you would pretend it had never happened.'

'Why should I?' he drawled with a half smile. 'From my point of view it was extremely enjoyable.'

Suddenly Nicola lost control and all the pent-up tension of the day took charge. With a strangled sound of pure rage she lifted her arm and hit Chris across the face.

The next moment she shrank back against the fridge, horrified at herself and at the same time shaking with fear because of what she saw in his eyes.

'No girl does that to me and gets away with it.' He spoke as though through clenched teeth. 'I'd like to put you across my knees and spank your bottom, but I've got a better punishment for you than that. Since you find my attentions so nauseating, no doubt you won't much care for being treated like this.'

His arms were round her and her head was being forced back until her throat felt stretched to choking point. His mouth thrust her lips apart until her heart pounded in her ears and she longed to be able to beg for mercy. And yet, at the same time a strange ecstasy possessed her and she wanted the embrace to go on for ever and ever.

It ended at last. Chris's arms dropped to his sides and Nicola, suddenly bereft of support, clutched at the back of a chair, her head drooping and her limbs weak with the force of her emotion.

'That's how a girl should be kissed.' He was breathing hard but the words came out clearly, intense with satisfaction and yet with a puzzling undercurrent of bitterness. 'But I'm afraid it wasn't much of a punishment for hitting me after all. You enjoy a bit of hot-blooded passion, don't you, Nicola? I'd better be off to my room before I forget we're not at that hotel on the front at Sandbeach.'

As she sank down on to the chair by the table she heard the door close behind him. But it was a long, long time before she recovered sufficiently to go to bed.

Morning came all too soon and Nicola's first sensation was one of dread. She didn't want to see Chris again until the memory of last night was a little less vivid, and it was an immense relief to find he had received an early call and gone off to deal with it. Alone in the flat, she started drearily on the chores.

When the phone rang just before she was due downstairs, she assumed it would be a medical call. To her delight it was her mother on the line.

'I shall be back this evening, dear. It was a very slight stroke, fortunately—more of a warning—and I think your grandfather will be sensible in future and not work so hard. How are things with you?'

'It's been great having Janet staying here but I shall be glad to see you back, all the same.' Nicola hesitated, wondering whether to mention her friend's accident. Before she could make up her mind Alison went on talking.

'You'll meet me at Debenbridge station, won't you, dear? The train gets in at seventeen-fifty, I think.'

That would fit in fairly well with visiting Janet and Nicola promised at once. They talked for a little longer and then rang off. Steeling herself for the coming meeting with Chris, she went downstairs.

It seemed like a reprieve when she discovered that he was still out.

'Where's Chris?' Dr Hardwick demanded when he realised that three of his assistant's patients were still in the waiting room.

'He's out on a maternity case,' Nicola told him. 'Mrs Greensmith's husband phoned about six o'clock. You remember she's a home delivery?'

'Yes. Goodness knows how long he'll be and he's needed here. It's extraordinary how much medical attention people require after a nice summer weekend.'

A few minutes later Dr Featherstone put his head out of his consulting room as Nicola was crossing the hall. 'Where's Chris?'

Nicola repeated the information she had already given her uncle, with much the same result except that the younger doctor had something to add.

'That young chap's settled down remarkably well in the practice and it's a damn nuisance that he'll be leaving soon. I suppose he still does want to do surgery, Nicola? You must have got to know him quite well since he moved into the flat.'

'He hasn't said anything about changing his mind.'

'James and I were talking it over the other day. We're both agreed that we must continue to employ an assistant and neither of us wants to make a fresh start with someone else. We might not be so lucky another time.' He smoothed back his pale thin hair and looked hopefully at Nicola. 'Couldn't you sound him out in a cautious sort of way?'

Well aware that Dr Hardwick would certainly not approve of such a circuitous route, Nicola smiled and shook her head. 'You'll have to ask him yourself, Doctor, but I don't think it would be a good idea to be too optimistic.'

Continuing on her way towards the dispensary to replenish her stock of bandages, she asked herself how she would feel about it if Chris did decide to stay. Would she be able to bear the bitter-sweetness of seeing him every day? Her heart had no difficulty in finding an answer, but her head was wiser and knew that it would be better to make a clean break.

Yet it was to her heart that she listened.

It was late before Chris returned. Finding that his patients had been dealt with, he snatched a cup of coffee and went out again immediately. Since he rarely came to the flat for lunch, Nicola felt fairly safe in planning to pack up Janet's things during her own lunch hour, and then turn out the bedroom in readiness for her mother's reoccupation.

At two-thirty she set out for the hospital, where she confidently expected to find Janet still in the sick bay. As she parked the Mini and walked towards the main entrance, Nicola was vividly reminded of her last visit when she had gone to see Chris.

So much had stemmed from that one afternoon. If she hadn't gone, Drs Hardwick and Featherstone would never have acquired Chris as an assistant, and she herself wouldn't be suffering her present heart-break.

Nicola sighed and abandoned such unprofitable thinking as she made her way to the nurses' sick bay. As she had guessed, Janet was still there, sitting in a comfortable chair with her bandaged foot on a stool. She was in a three-bedded ward but the other two patients were well surrounded by visitors and there was no difficulty about talking quietly together.

'They won't let me go until the swelling is reduced,' Janet said. 'Not that I mind—I'm quite happy here and rather enjoying being waited on. It'll be great for a day or two but I expect I shall get restless after that. How are things at Moresham?'

'Okay.' Nicola unfastened the case she had brought and began to take out the toilet articles and other items she had carefully packed on top. 'I expect you'll be glad to get into one of your own nighties.'

'Will you tell your mother you were alone with Chris last night?'

Nicola laughed. 'How shocking that sounds! Yes, I expect I shall break it to her at a suitable moment. I'm going to meet her when I leave here.'

'Talking of Chris,' Janet said. 'Does he know about Mr Bradshaw?'

'What about him?' Nicola stared at her, sitting back on her heels.

'You don't know either? You can't have seen the local paper then. It's sprawled across the front page of the lunch-time edition.' She bent to retrieve it from beside her chair. 'Here you are. *Well-known Surgeon Killed*. They seem to think he had a heart attack at the wheel of his car but they won't know definitely until the post-mortem. It's strange, isn't it, that he was a heart specialist?'

'Very strange,' Nicola said absently, taking the

paper from her and scanning the short paragraphs under big black capitals. 'Oh, Janet—how absolutely awful! He was only in his fifties and such a brilliant surgeon. Chris will be terribly upset.'

'Perhaps you'll have to tell him. I don't envy you.'

'I shouldn't think so. He'll be bound to have picked up the news on his round.'

They discussed it for some time, but even after they had gone on to another subject it was very much in the forefront of Nicola's mind. She forgot it for a short time when she went to meet her mother, who was full of news about her stay in Yorkshire, but she remembered it again as soon as they reached the doctor's house.

It was half-way through the evening surgery and Chris was busy. Although Nicola looked anxiously at him she could detect nothing out of the ordinary in his expression.

'I've got a lot to do this evening,' he told her curtly later on, 'so I shan't be in for the meal. I'll get some food in a pub.' And he was gone before she could even answer him.

Her mother went to bed early, tired out, but Nicola continued to sit before the television screen, its coloured pictures flitting unseen before her eyes. At eleven o'clock she heard Chris coming up the stairs, but instead of taking them slowly and despondently—as she would have expected—he was bounding up two at a time.

The puzzle was quickly solved. He was in a very bad temper.

'Why didn't you tell me?' he demanded, storming into the sitting-room. 'You must have known because the evening paper is lying on the hall table and I remember seeing it there when I came in at surgery time. Yet you didn't say a word, and if it hadn't been for a heart patient mentioning Bradshaw's death I might still not have known about it.'

'There wasn't time. You were in a hurry to start surgery and you went rushing out immediately afterwards.'

'It would have taken no more than two seconds. There was time enough.' He stood before her, his hands on his hips and his eyes hot with anger. 'I suppose you thought you'd got to break the news gently—give me time to recover before facing my patient—all that rubbish. I'm not Steve, you know—I don't need taking care of—and I've told you before that I strongly object to being mothered.'

'It's stupid to talk like that.' Nicola tried to whip up her anger to equal his, but could manage nothing stronger than indignation. Chris always seemed to be angry with her now, she thought unhappily. 'I meant it for the best,' she finished quietly.

'No doubt you did, but I don't think much of your judgment.' Chris flung himself into an armchair and leaned back wearily. 'It's a hell of a thing to happen, whichever way you look at it.

He was a thoroughly nice guy and I liked him immensely, added to which he was brilliant at his job and there isn't another local man to touch him. Besides, there's my own point of view. I'd been congratulating myself on having the post held for me—it sure was a lucky break—and I'd been really looking forward to starting work at the hospital.'

'I'd rather got the impression that you liked general practice better than you'd expected,' Nicola ventured.

'You what?' He stared at her. 'Well, maybe I do, but that doesn't mean I want to spend my life doing it.'

'You've been very successful, though, and my uncle is quite sold on the idea of having an assistant.'

She was doing exactly what Dr Featherstone had suggested, she realised suddenly—sounding Chris out. Not that it mattered, for he obviously hadn't listened to a word. He had left his chair and was restlessly pacing up and down the room.

'I think I'd better go up to the hospital at the first possible moment and find out what the prospects are. Somebody will have to take over as senior heart surgeon and perhaps he'll be willing to take me on as registrar.' He paused and braced his shoulders. 'It's all quite simple really, and very likely I haven't anything to worry about at all.'

Nicola repressed a sigh and said a quick good night. As she went to her room she was torn by the conflicting emotions which seemed to be becoming a habit. She wanted Chris to have his chance, but the thought that he would go right out of her life was unbearably painful. In the meantime, there was nothing she could do to influence the outcome. She would simply have to wait and see like everyone else.

It wasn't easy, though, particularly as no one said anything to her on the subject—except for her mother, who said a great deal but had no more power than she had herself to affect the course of events.

'I hope Chris decides to stay.' Alison was very definite about that. 'James might not find another young doctor who suits him so well—he might even refuse to get another assistant and then we'd be back to square one, with both partners rushed off their feet.'

'Chris hasn't been offered a permanent job here yet,' Nicola felt impelled to point out.

'But he's going to be.'

Nicola's heart leapt. 'How do you know? Did Uncle tell you?'

Alison shook her head. 'Not him. It was Peter Featherstone when I happened to meet him as I was going out shopping this morning.'

They were talking on the evening following her return from Yorkshire. The table was laid, as usual, for three and they awaited Chris's appearance. He had finished surgery; Nicola knew that because she had seen the last patient leave. But he had not immediately followed her upstairs.

'We'll give him five more minutes,' Alison said, 'and then make a start. I'm not having our food spoilt as well as his.'

He came a moment later and made straight for the big comfortable kitchen where they always ate their meals, but he did not immediately sit down. Instead he closed the door behind him and leaned back against it, his expression unusually tense.

'Come along, Chris,' Alison ordered him briskly. 'You're late enough already.'

'Afraid I'd forgotten about food.' He gave her a faint apologetic smile. 'I've got rather a lot on my mind at the moment and meals have got pushed into the background.'

'Did you have any lunch?'

'There wasn't time. I went into Debenbridge instead. I had an appointment at the hospital.'

'About your arm?'

'What?' He looked at her in astonishment and then glanced down at his left arm which hung rather stiffly, the lightweight plaster hidden under the sleeve of his jacket. 'No, no, nothing to do with that. I'm not due at the orthopaedic clinic again yet.'

Nicola moistened dry lips. 'It was about the job, wasn't it? You had to find out where you stood.'

'Yes,' said Chris, 'I had to find out.'

CHAPTER THIRTEEN

THE SILENCE seemed to last for ever but eventually Alison said impatiently, 'Well, go on, Chris. Tell us what happened.'

Chris moved away from the door and sat down at the table. Looking at him anxiously, Nicola noted the signs of strain; there was a sombreness in his eyes and a tightness round the mouth. But his voice when he spoke was deliberately casual.

'I saw the bloke who's expecting to step into Bradshaw's shoes. He was very friendly and courteous—apologetic almost—but he made it quite clear that the arrangement which his ex-boss had made with me was a personal thing, no longer valid. The registrar who's been doing the job I hoped to take over wants to stay on and will very likely become a junior consultant. That means a general move upwards all down the line.'

'Oh dear.' Once more it was Alison who carried on the conversation. 'You must have been terribly disappointed.'

Nicola wouldn't have dared to say that. He would have immediately accused her of 'mothering' him, but he could take it from an older woman, though he only shrugged in reply.

'It wasn't altogether a surprise, was it, Chris?'

she ventured to ask.

His eyes met hers briefly. 'No, of course not, but one always hopes.'

Alison had turned away to dish up the meal and the subject was dropped, though no one seemed to have very much to say in its place. In spite of his abstraction Chris ate hungrily and Nicola would have given a great deal to be allowed a glimpse of his thoughts. She doubted whether he entirely believed the account he had given of his rejection at Debenbridge General. It sounded phoney to her and she wondered if the unnamed surgeon had ever heard of him before.

In view of Mr Bradshaw's well-known autocratic ways it seemed probable that he had not taken the other surgeons who worked with him into his confidence.

Not that any of it mattered now. Chris had reached a crossroads in his career, when some decision must be made regarding the future.

He lost no time in making it.

Two days later Dr Hardwick called Nicola into his consulting room as soon as he arrived. 'Don't let Chris go off on his round without seeing me first and, if possible, Dr Featherstone as well.' Seeing the question in her eyes, he added in a businesslike tone, 'We have a proposition to make to him which I hope he will find attractive.'

'You're offering him a permanent job?'

'Exactly, with a view to partnership eventually. If he's got any sense he won't turn it down.'

Nicola did not venture to comment on that.

There was a crying child in the waiting room and she went to find out what was the matter.

A little girl of about six, with large, frightened eyes, was clutching a smaller boy by the hand. He had a dirty handkerchief wrapped round his palm, through which the blood was already oozing.

'Sean cut hisself,' the girl explained. 'With the bread knife.'

'However did he manage to get hold of it? And where's your mum?'

'He snatched it off the table and Mum said I'd got to bring him cos she'd be late for work.'

Nicola accepted the information without further questioning, and took the children off to the room where she dealt with such matters. The cut was not deep and required no stitching, but after it had been cleaned up and plastered she spent some time restoring both children to a happier frame of mind.

She was crossing the hall, holding a hand of each, when she met Chris. It seemed a good moment to deliver her uncle's message.

'Very well, provided I don't have to dash off to an emergency.' He looked down at Sean and rumpled his thatch of fair hair. 'Everything okay with these two?'

Sensing a kindly interest, the little girl burst out into the story of the bread knife. 'But Nurse has made it all better,' she finished triumphantly.

'She enjoys that sort of thing, but people don't always appreciate it as much as you do.' Seeing her look of bewilderment, he laughed and returned to his room.

Nicola despatched the two children to their home and got on with her work. As the time began to fly past she both longed for and dreaded the coming meeting between the three doctors. One moment she hoped desperately that Chris would accept the offer of a permanent job, the next she told herself firmly that it would be far better all round if he went right away, out of her life.

No emergency cropped up to send him driving off to deal with it. Surgery hour ended and Dr Featherstone appeared and went into Dr Hardwick's room. Chris joined them almost at once and the door was firmly closed.

'It's not hard to guess what's going on in there,' Mrs Robson said.

Nicola glanced at the receptionist, noting automatically that her unnaturally dark hair was blacker than ever. 'Isn't it?' she said cautiously.

'Come off it, dear! I bet you know all about it, Dr Hardwick being your uncle. They're offering him a job—am I right?' Pausing for a reply and receiving none, she added curiously, 'Or maybe it's a partnership?'

'I think we'll have to wait and see what happens, Mrs Robson.' With relief Nicola remembered the untidy waiting room. 'I'd better get on. I want to make some calls before lunch.'

Ignoring an offended sniff she began to pick up comics and toys, to straighten chairs and rescue plants pushed out of place. There was a murmur of voices coming from the next room but she could not even distinguish one from another. Fortunately she wasn't kept long in suspense. A door opened and Chris strode past the waiting room, and almost at once she heard the sound of his car starting up.

Nicola told herself that such a rapid departure *might* indicate a quick acceptance, the details to be discussed later. And it could just as easily mean that Chris had refused outright and saw no point in continuing the interview.

'Silly young fool!' snapped Dr Hardwick, appearing suddenly in the doorway. 'Doesn't know when he's well off.'

'I must say I was hopeful—very hopeful,' came Dr Featherstone's voice from behind him.

'So was I, but it's no good, Peter. We shall have to start looking out for a replacement.'

'So long as you're willing to do that, I don't mind so much. Personally, I couldn't stand going back to the old days with just the two of us working ourselves to death.'

'Wouldn't he even consider it?' Nicola asked.

'He would not.' Dr Hardwick glared at her as though it had been her fault. 'It seems he's made up his mind to go to London and has even started applying for jobs. He hasn't wasted much time.'

She turned away, her arms full of magazines and her heart overflowing with despair. Now that she definitely knew Chris was leaving she knew with miserable certainty exactly how much she had wanted him to stay.

The next two weeks were desperately unhappy, made all the worse because Nicola knew she must hide it from everyone. Alison thought she was overtired and needed a holiday, urging her to go up to Yorkshire in the early autumn. Chris ignored her whenever he could without making it obvious, and spent a great deal of time in his own sitting-room, writing letters which he went out early to post in the morning.

She guessed that they were applications for registrar's posts in London.

One day he went into Debenbridge and returned triumphant without his plaster. His arm, he admitted, was still a little stiff but he intended to exercise it as much as possible and it would soon recover completely.

'Fortunately I've always kept my fingers flexed,' he told Alison. 'I should have no problems at all when I take up surgery again.'

'You think that will be soon?'

'I hope so. I've got a couple of interviews to attend next week, as a matter of fact. Both are good jobs and I don't really mind which one I get offered.'

'I expect you'll be lucky,' she said, a little wistfully. 'You've got what it takes.'

'I hope so.' Chris smiled and bent his head to kiss her impulsively on the cheek. 'Keep your fingers crossed for me, Alison. It's so desperately important.'

To Nicola he said nothing at all.

But she did manage to exchange a word with

him before he left for London. They met by
chance on the landing, Nicola still in her dressing-gown and Chris correctly dressed in a dark
suit. He already had, it seemed to her, an aura of
success. His well-brushed hair gleamed and his
skin was tanned and healthy-looking; the ex-
pensive suit had obviously been made for him
and fitted perfectly.

Nevertheless, she felt constrained to offer her
good wishes. 'I hope all goes well for you and that
you—you get what you want.'

He gave her a long stare. 'Does anyone ever
get that?' At the top of the stairs he paused with
his hand on the newel post. 'Will you tell your
mother, please, that I shall be very late back. I
have a Canadian friend at one of the hospitals I'm
visiting and we're spending the evening together.
Don't put the catch on the door unless you want
to be disturbed in the middle of the night.'

The day seemed endless. Fortunately it was
the one on which Nicola held her clinic for expectant mothers and she always enjoyed that. It
was particularly interesting on this occasion, for
among the chattering crowd in the waiting room
she discovered Mrs Riley, the young woman who
had tried to commit suicide. Chris had visited her
after she came out of hospital and her record card
showed that she had made a good recovery.

'Thought I'd better come along and get myself
checked up seeing as I'm three months gone
now,' she told Nicola, tilting her head defiantly.
'So I left Gary with my Mum and here I am.'

Her hair was elaborately arranged and was an over-all blonde without any dark roots. That alone was sufficient to tell Nicola that she was now in a happier frame of mind.

'How have you been feeling, Mrs Riley?' she asked.

'Not too bad at all. Much better than last time.'

So that was that, and Nicola was more than ever thankful that they had been in time to save her from the effects of her previous despair. Greatly cheered by the encounter, she worked her way through the clinic and then plunged into evening surgery.

Her working day ended at last but there was still the evening to get through. Fortunately Janet rang up with time to kill and they talked for some while. She had been back on the ward for more than two weeks and seemed almost to have forgotten her sprain. Nor did she say anything about Chris and Nicola did not mention him either.

He was very much in her thoughts when she went to bed and she found sleep elusive. The weather was sultry and she flung her window wide, but still the room felt hot and stuffy and she tossed and turned.

Eventually she drifted into a doze which developed into deep slumber. Time ceased to exist and unhappiness was forgotten in the healing depths of unconsciousness.

Hours later—or so it seemed—she was suddenly wide awake again. Some sound had disturbed her and her sleep-drugged mind had registered it as the faint tinkle of glass. Convinced that she must be wrong about that, she nevertheless felt impelled to get out of bed and cross to the window. Her room was at the back and below it the extension to the dispensary jutted out into the garden.

It had a flat roof with a skylight, and from this there came a weak, wavering light.

Nicola's first thought was a terrifying one. Fire! She snatched her dressing-gown and thrust her arms into it as she ran from the room. Was Chris back yet? She longed to find out but dared not stop. With the speed of daily familiarity she raced down the stairs and turned towards the back of the house. The inner doors were always kept locked at night, so as not to make things too easy for intruders, and the dispensary door faced her, its solid Victorian mahogany a formidable barrier to whatever—or whoever—was on the other side.

If she didn't open it she wouldn't find out. Summoning all her courage, Nicola turned the key and swung the door wide.

It wasn't fire after all. The wavering light came from a torch held in someone's hand and a giant shadow wobbled over the walls and the glass doors of cupboards, dark, featureless and terrifying. In one of the windows overlooking the garden a black patch showed where a pane had been cut out.

The door had creaked slightly—as it always

did—and suddenly the torch beam shone straight at Nicola, blinding her so effectively that the person behind it became invisible. With an instinctive gesture she put up her hand to shield her eyes and at the same moment the light advanced towards her at vicious speed. There was a horrible, sickening crack and a stinging pain in her head. With a moan she slumped against the door post, clutching at it helplessly and vaguely aware of someone forcing a way past her and into the hall.

As she slid to the floor and lapsed into unconsciousness she heard the front door opening.

Her return to life was slow and reluctant and for a moment she couldn't remember why she was lying on the floor downstairs in the middle of the night, nor why her head ached so unbearably. There was a warm, wet feeling on her forehead and something trickled into her left eye. She gave a little whimper of pain and it turned into a sob.

'Oh, Nicola—Nicola darling—don't cry! You're quite safe now.' Strong arms gathered her tenderly into a warm embrace. 'Just lie still for a few minutes.'

It was Chris's voice. Nicola's eyes flew open and she looked straight up into his face, her own gaze totally bewildered.

'You—you called me darling,' she said weakly. 'Or did I dream it?'

'It was no dream, love, and if you'd rather I hadn't said it, then it's just too bad.' His tone was suddenly bitter. 'God knows I've wanted to say it long enough and in tonight's rather exceptional circumstances it slipped out. I'm afraid it's gone beyond recall.'

'But I don't want you to recall it!' Driven by the force of her emotions she tried to sit up but subsided against his arm with a groan. 'Say it again, Chris—please—'

'What?' He stared incredulously into her face. 'You can't mean it—'

'But I do!' Dizzy with the force of the blow she had received, she was still clear-headed enough to grasp that somehow a miracle had happened and the Chris, who had lately seemed so stand-offish and even cruel, had changed unbelievably into someone tender and loving.

'I don't understand. I thought Steve coming back like that had spoilt everything. You nursed him so devotedly—'

'You made me,' she interrupted.

'I wanted you to be sure of your own feelings— and I thought you *were* sure, but I got it wrong, didn't I?' And when she confirmed it, he went on passionately, 'I've loved you for such a long time but things kept going wrong and I came to the conclusion that you couldn't stand me. Besides, I didn't really want to fall in love with you or anybody else. After the Canadian girl ditched me I made up my mind it wasn't going to happen again. I'd planned a dead straight route to the top careerwise and I reckoned I'd travel faster on my own.'

'I expect you would too,' she said, her voice quivering a little.

'And be hellish lonely doing it.'

'I still can't really believe that—that you love me. Would you mind saying it again?'

'I love you, love you, love you—' His arms tightened around her. 'And I shan't stop kissing you until you believe it.'

The pain in her head forgotten, Nicola surrendered to the utter bliss of being held in Chris's arms and feeling in her own body the pounding of his heart as strongly as though they were indeed one person. An emotion more powerful than anything she had ever experienced before swept through her so that her one urgent desire was to give and receive the tender, passionate proof of love.

It was a long time before they drew apart, to lie quietly for a moment on the hard floor. And then Chris said huskily, 'You will marry me, won't you, darling, and come to London with me?'

'To London? You got a job then?'

'Both of them.' He smiled. 'But I only want one and I chose the post with the best prospects. You haven't answered my question.'

Nicola's answer was swift and eminently satisfactory, and there was another interval before they returned to the present.

'We really must do something about your head,' Chris said at last. 'It's stopped bleeding so I think the cut is only superficial, but it must be properly attended to.'

'I suppose the intruder hit me with his torch.' She glanced round and discovered it lying in a corner with the light still switched on. 'Did you see him, Chris? Or were you too late?'

'I opened the front door and walked right into him. It wasn't difficult to size up the situation but I was too concerned about you to grapple with him. It didn't matter because I'd already recognised him.'

Nicola stared at him. 'Really? Whoever was it?'

'Do you remember that accident outside on my first morning? It was the motor cyclist. I expect he was after drugs. I found him wandering about the place after the accident, you know, and I was a bit suspicious of him then.'

'I'm not sure if we have a record of his name and address—'

'Doesn't matter. We sent him up to the hospital for a check-up and they'll have the details. The police will probably pick him up quite easily.'

'I suppose we should be grateful to him,' Nicola said slowly, 'but I don't much care for the idea.'

'Then forget it. What does it matter *how* we came together?' Chris kissed her tenderly. 'The important thing is that we *are* together and nothing and nobody is ever going to come between us again.'

His work almost certainly would, Nicola thought fleetingly, but she did not let it worry her. She was a nurse and she understood. She hoped that she would always understand.

Doctor Nurse Romances